PRICE OF FREEDOM

THE BAD COMPANY™ BOOK THREE

CRAIG MARTELLE

MICHAEL ANDERLE

DISRUPTIVE IMAGINATION®

PRICE OF FREEDOM

We can't write without those who support us
On the home front, we thank you for being
there for us

We wouldn't be able to do this for a living if it weren't for our
readers
We thank you for reading our books

PRICE OF FREEDOM TEAM

Thanks to the JIT Readers

James Caplan
Kimberly Boyer
Timothy Bischoff
Peter Manis
Micky Cocker
Paul Westman
Kelly O'Donnell
John Ashmore
Veronica Torres

If I've missed anyone, please let me know!

Editor
Mia Darien, www.miadarien.com

CHARACTERS & TIMELINE

World's Worst Day Ever (WWDE)

WWDE + 20 years, Terry Henry returns from self-imposed exile. The Terry Henry Walton Chronicles detail his adventures from that time to WWDE+150

WWDE + 150 years – Michael returns to Earth. BA returns to Earth. TH & Char go to space

Key Players

- Terry Henry Walton (was forty-five on the WWDE)—called TH by his friends. Enhanced with nanocytes by Bethany Anne herself, wears the rank of Colonel, leads the Force de Guerre (FDG), a military unit that he established on WWDE+20
- Charumati (was sixty-five on the WWDE)—A Werewolf, married to Terry, carries the rank of Major in the FDG

- Kimber (born WWDE+15, adopted approximately WWDE+25 by TH & Char, enhanced on WWDE+65)—Major in the FDG
- Her husband Auburn Weathers (enhanced on WWDE+82)—provides logistics support to the FDG
- Kaeden (born WWDE+16, adopted approximately WWDE+24 by TH & Char, enhanced on WWDE+65)—Major in the FDG
- His wife Marcie Spires (born on WWDE+22, naturally enhanced)—Colonel in the FDG
- Cory (born WWDE+25, naturally enhanced, gifted with the power to heal)
- Her husband Ramses—Major in the FDG

Vampires

- Joseph (born three hundred years before the WWDE)
- Petricia (born WWDE+30)

Pricolici (Werewolves that walk upright)

- Nathan Lowell (President of the Bad Company and Bethany Anne's Chief of Intelligence)
- Ecaterina (Nathan's spouse)
- Christina (Nathan & Ecaterina's daughter)

Werewolves

- Sue & Timmons (long-term members of Char's pack)
- Shonna & Merrit (long-term members of Char's pack)
- Ted (with Felicity, an enhanced human)

Weretigers born before the WWDE:

- Aaron & Yanmei

Humans (enhanced)

- Micky San Marino, Captain of the *War Axe*
- Commander Suresha, *War Axe* Department Head – Engines
- Commander MacEachthighearna (Mac), *War Axe* Department Head—Environmental
- Commander Blagun Lagunov, *War Axe* Department—Structure
- Commander Oscar Wirth, *War Axe* Department Head—Stores
- Lieutenant Clodagh Shortall, *War Axe* engine technician
- Sergeant Fitzroy, a martial arts expert and platoon sergeant
- Kelly, Capples, Fleeter, Praeter, & Duncan— mech drivers

Other Key Characters

- Dokken (a sentient German Shepherd)

- The Good King Wenceslaus (an orange tabby who thinks he's a weretiger, all fifteen pounds of him)
- K'thrall—a Yollin who works on the bridge of the *War Axe*
- Clifton—human pilot of the *War Axe*
- Bundin—a four-legged shell-backed stalk-headed blue alien from Poddern
- Ankh'Po'Turn—a small bald humanoid from Crenellia
- General Smedley Butler – EI/AI on the War Axe, who they call the general
- Plato – Ted's AI from R&D
- Dionysus – the AI tasked to assist with running Keeg Station

CHAPTER ONE

Keeg Station

"We need more intel, Nathan," Terry Henry Walton told the image on the monitor.

"Life or death struggle, the security of the universe, the Queen needs it? How many different ways do I have to say that this one is non-negotiable?"

"We're two for two in shitstorms, and I'd like to break that streak. We want on-the-ground intelligence so we can get inside their heads before they get into ours." Terry ran a hand through his hair—which was getting long—and shook his head, imagining a lion's mane. He turned his attention back to the screen. "Once we're in orbit, we'll collect intel and plan our attack before we get thrown into the middle of someone else's mess."

"It's no one's mess, TH." Nathan waved at the colonel to calm him.

"The Benitons *didn't* cause this by messing around with a miniaturized Etheric power source?" Terry looked down his nose at Nathan.

"That hasn't been confirmed." Nathan leaned forward, his face filling Terry's screen.

"Nice passive voice, Nathan. Like I said, we'll go in before the month's out and clean up someone else's mess, but we're not going to race to our own demise. I am amazed we didn't get anyone killed out here. I know how to fight a battle—hell, a whole *war*—but I feel like I don't know jack shit now that we're in space. Micro-sized explosives, tanks that cover a city block, unmanned wars. Son of a bitch, Nathan!" Terry's gaze swept the room, as if someone might have snuck into his and Char's quarters when he wasn't looking, then with his hand over his mouth, he said, "I might be in over my head."

"Nonsense! No one else would have had a chance on those last two missions. You made chicken salad, my friend, and you'll do the same thing in this next engagement. These creatures need to go back to where they came from. We don't want them in our universe. We need to keep them from establishing a foothold on Benitus Seven."

"They already *have* a foothold, so now we have to drive a determined enemy from a battlefield of their choosing." Terry gritted his teeth. "MORE INTEL!"

"I expect you'll choose the battlefield. Even if you don't think you are, you are. They won't know what hit them. If there's nothing else, Nathan Lowell, signing off." The screen went dark before Terry could reply.

He sat down on the bed with little intention of leaving his quarters on Keeg Station. After their arrival, Ted had made a beeline for Felicity and Terry had run for his life. He had not left his quarters since.

That had been two days ago.

He thought about taking another shower, but decided against it. He hadn't worked out since they'd been here. He hung his head between his knees. TH did not want to leave his quarters, but he had to. Everything he wanted to do was out there, beyond the door.

"This is crazy! It's only Felicity." He stood up and marched to the door, but stopped short. "Only. Felicity."

He looked at the door, chuckling at his conundrum. Neither he nor the door moved. "Ted might have a point. *Damn.* She's going to tear me a new asshole. Come on, one foot in front of the other. Go take your medicine."

But I don't have to take it alone, Terry thought. He accessed his comm chip. *My lover, are you there?*

Are you? Charumati replied.

Ouch!

Come out to the promenade. Felicity is waiting, and she's got Ted by the ear. I'll make it worth your while, Char crooned.

Terry wasn't sure, but thought he heard purring. *Is Dokken with you?*

Of course. We're all here, waiting on you. Come on, TH. We have stuff to do. It's only Felicity.

I tried that argument already, and it didn't work. But all right. I'm coming.

Terry took a deep breath and tapped the access panel, and the door opened. He stuck his head out and looked both ways down the residential corridor as if expecting an ambush, but no one was there so he stepped out, then strode briskly toward the lift to take him to the deck with the shops. He wondered what treasures his family had acquired this trip...and he wondered how angry Felicity was.

Maybe she could channel her angst against the red devils on Benitus Seven. He was still chuckling when the lift's door opened.

Felicity's sour expression instantly turned hostile. "What's so funny?" she demanded. Terry's family and the pack were arrayed around her as if watching a prizefight. He gave them all the stink-eye before turning to Felicity and delivering his most winning smile.

"You look magnificent!" TH told her, but he couldn't help himself. "You don't look a day over a hundred."

"WHAT?" she howled.

"I don't understand," Ted said softly. "You are well over a hundred years old."

She turned on him. "You shut up." She stabbed a finger repeatedly in his direction. He looked at it clinically, but didn't say anything further. She swiveled her head casually and locked her eyes on the colonel.

He pursed his lips and looked anywhere but at Felicity. Someone behind her snorted. Felicity held two fingers over her shoulder, pointer pressed against thumb. *Zip it.*

Terry looked for support, but the response from the peanut gallery was less than overwhelming. At least twenty of his family and friends were in view. "Come on," Terry pleaded. "Not a single one of you?"

Headshakes or blank looks.

"That should tell you all you need to know, Terry Henry Walton." Felicity continued to glare.

"No one will take a bullet for me. Check."

Felicity's lip twitched.

"Not a day over a hundred," TH whispered.

"By all that's holy and the nine levels of Hell…"

"It's nine *circles* of Hell," Terry interjected.

"All the levels of Hell!" Felicity continued, face as red as if it were on fire. "You almost got my husband killed!"

Terry opened his mouth, but nothing came out. He couldn't argue with her—not about that—because he thought she was right.

Her lower lip started to tremble.

"No... Don't."

The tears started to flow, followed by sobbing. Ted looked as uncomfortable as Terry Henry felt. TH pulled her into a hug but she resisted, pounding on his chest with both hands.

Ted started to move away, but Char grabbed his arm and held on. He pulled weakly, but she held him in place.

Felicity gave in and let Terry embrace her. His eyes glistened, and he blinked rapidly.

After Felicity pushed herself away, she shook one finger at TH in warning. "Don't you ever do that again! You are responsible for him, so you keep him safe." She wrapped her arm around Ted's and ushered him away.

Char hurried to Terry and put her arms around his neck. "You can handle getting shot at—even getting shot— but you break down into a blubbering mess whenever there's a crying woman?"

"And needles, but thank the fucking stars for the apocalypse! We don't have any more of those."

A nearby mother covered her toddler's ears and glared at Terry Henry. He wondered for only a moment.

"Oh, shit! I'm sorry, ma'am." The woman picked her son up and hurried off. "That's it. This is a family station, so I'm going to swear off swearing!"

Terry's voice carried. Kim and Kae looked at each other and started to laugh, then pointed at their dad and laughed even harder. Dokken appeared, wagging his tail, and looked up at Terry.

That was the funniest shit I've seen all day, the dog told him.

"Is it that unbelievable that I could go without swearing?" Terry held his hands out to the assembled group. The werewolves shook their heads, and Cordelia approached and slapped her father on his shoulder.

"The word you're looking for is 'inconceivable.' Ramses is taking bets over there on how long you'll last."

Terry looked over Cory's shoulder at her husband, who was making annotations in a small notebook.

"I'll be damned," TH said.

"See? You can't help yourself." Cory called, *"Time!"* and Ramses threw his hands up in frustration.

"Come on, TH! No one thought you'd lose it this soon. Do over," he declared, and started writing again.

"It is a tall mountain you've set out to climb, but I'm here for you," Char said, her purple eyes twinkling under the artificial lights of the shopping level.

"I could ask for no better support for my journey to clean living."

"For shame, Terry Henry," Christina said as she walked by with the werewolves.

"Bullshit," Timmons murmured from the back of the pack.

Terry resisted the urge to give him the finger.

"Yes, that counts," Char declared.

Terry curled his lip. Sometimes his wife read his mind.

He was convinced she was a telepath, but in all the time they'd been together she'd never admitted it. "How about dinner? Just us. I don't want to look at any of these turncoats!"

"They are not turncoats." Char waved the others away with a smile and the group broke up, each couple heading in a different direction. Only Ankh'Po'Turn and Bundin remained. Terry hadn't noticed them before.

Ankh looked at Terry and Char for a few moments before heading toward the lift.

"Going to the lab, buddy?" Terry asked. The Crenellian waved over his shoulder. "What about you, Bundin? Where are Joseph and Petricia?"

"They were supposed to meet me here. They will be disappointed that they missed the show," the Podder replied.

Terry clamped his mouth shut and closed his eyes.

Joseph, are you on your way to the promenade? Char asked over her comm chip.

"Just arriving now. No! Don't tell me we missed it?" Joseph replied, looking at Petricia for sympathy.

"It was epic," Char told them. "TH has sworn off swearing, too."

"No kidding? Good for you, Terry Henry Walton. I always thought you were far too educated for such language. Gentlemen simply do not speak that way," Joseph said, his natural British accent adding emphasis.

Terry's hand quivered. It wanted once again to dial up a middle finger, but he held it down.

"We're going for dinner, and you can't come," he said, raising his head.

"Don't be Dickensian," came Joseph's retort. "We were on our way to the Seppukarian place. They say it twists one's stomach so much it feels like you're committing seppuku."

Terry looked closely into Joseph's eyes. "I think he's serious."

Char nodded in agreement.

"Come on, Bundin, tell us all about this epic throwdown we missed..." Joseph, Petricia, and Bundin ambled away.

Somewhere Deep in the Etheric Federation

Nathan stood up from his desk, pumping his fist in triumph. "*R2D2* does it again!"

He pointed to the computer screen, where a three-dimensional image of a Pepsi container rotated. The image morphed to Coke before his eyes.

The next shipment was on its way through the core of the Federation, hidden in plain sight.

Ecaterina strolled in, catching him mid-celebration. "Are you ready?" she asked, eyeing him critically. "What is going on here?"

"I'd rather have Coke!" Nathan declared.

"No, you wouldn't," Ecaterina replied, confused. Nathan spun the monitor around and replayed the image.

"It's something they developed on *R2D2*—a chip-controlled paint that arranges itself into images. This is a container vessel of Pepsi, but it'll look like Coke in transit." Nathan smiled broadly, showing his straight white teeth.

"I love it! A lifetime supply delivered uninterrupted... but what if someone drinks some?"

"Pretenders wouldn't know the difference, only the true connoisseurs."

"All this to sneak in some damn Pepsi?" Ecaterina cocked one hip and looked sideways at her husband. You know that BA lifted the ban on Pepsi and allocated all profits to support the Direct Action Branch, so why the feigned subterfuge?"

"Yes. I think the Queen is onto me."

"She's not here and there's nothing to be onto!" Ecaterina crossed her arms.

Nathan tapped the side of his nose. "That damn woman has eyes and ears everywhere."

Ecaterina rolled her eyes. "It's time to go. There's a play in the station theater— a real play—and you agreed to go!"

"Pepsi with a Coke label. It's genius, but you know me. Subterfuge is my thing. I'm sorry. I did notice that you look great! Let me grab my..." He looked for something to take. "I guess I don't need anything, do I?"

She shook her head.

"Did you see that? Pepsi, coming right in under their Coke-loving noses."

"That could be misinterpreted," Ecaterina replied.

"Yes, yes, of course," Nathan conceded. "You'll have your Pepsi, and you can drink it too."

Nathan could get a Coke anytime he wanted, but there were advantages to Ecaterina thinking he was converting. And the market could use a little encouragement, to bump up the profits in both areas. He had to fund the next Direct Action Branch operation from Pepsi and other Bad

Company sources, just until they could incorporate the miniaturized Etheric power supply. Then the cost of Direct Action Branch operations would be irrelevant.

He shut his computer down, walked around his desk, and offered his arm, then Nathan and Ecaterina strolled casually from his office.

CHAPTER TWO

Kaeden looked over the new suits. Only four again, but the Direct Action Branch had not been gone that long. To Kae, each mission was a lifetime. The colonel wanted powered, armored suits for everyone.

The value of the suits had been proven in the first missions. Unfortunately, there was no operational pause in which to improve their weaponry. There wouldn't be any new Jean Dukes Specials, either. Those took far longer than a week to manufacture, and the process didn't take place on Keeg Station.

Kae shook his head.

"What's wrong?" Daniel asked with concern. He followed Kaeden's eyes to the joints of one of the suits and hurried to it, looking for whatever defect Kae was seeing.

"Only four suits, that's what's wrong. These things are incredible. Make us feel invincible against every enemy, but the power ran out and that bit us on the dark planet. We weren't engaged long enough for that to be a problem in the last op. And now we're going to a place where we may find a power source for these things that is infinite. Can you imagine that?"

Daniel, who was the station's logistics chief, leaned against the suit. "I *can* imagine that. If you bring the power supply back, the engineers here will adapt it and we'll upgrade the suits when we get some time. Your deployment schedule is killer!"

Auburn appeared from the armory area of the logistics center and handed a pad to Daniel.

"That's what we'll need delivered to the *War Axe*." Auburn tapped the screen. "Got any more rockets?"

"What you see is what we have. We made sure to stock everything that cleared production, so we'll get your reloads moving."

Auburn smirked when he looked at Kae.

"That bad, huh?" Kae asked.

"Yup. I think we may have had it better on Earth."

Kae vigorously shook his head and pointed with both hands at the suits. "Look at these babies! We may not be maxed on our loadouts, but these things know no fear."

"Just because you've been successful so far doesn't mean the next enemy won't jack you up."

"That cuts me, brother." Kae laughed. "I know what you're saying. Just when I embrace my immortality someone will drop a nuke on our heads—but I won't know I'm gone."

"What nonsense are you spewing?" Marcie asked from the doorway.

"Nothing!" Kae replied quickly.

"Listen, Major, it's not my job to put you into a hopeless situation. Trust me."

Kae wrapped his arms around his wife's waist. "Yes, Colonel, but there's always something we don't know. You wouldn't throw us into the middle of the shit if you had a choice, or if you knew they had ballbusters like nukes."

"And I'd be right there with you. Which suit is mine?" Marcie replied, looking over her husband's shoulder as he nuzzled her neck.

"Nuuumpff," he said.

She pushed him to arm's length. "Say that again."

"None of them," he replied softly, looking into her eyes.

"Fine." She turned to Daniel. "When will more suits be ready?"

"We're churning out four a week, but we'll be out of raw materials after the next four. Shipment due in a month, start again, four per week. You still need thirty-two or something like that, so say about four months."

"How in the hell does that come to four months?" Marcie wondered, ticking the numbers off her fingers. Auburn was mumbling the math to himself.

"Raw material shipments are every other month, maybe even every third month. I prefer to under-promise and over-deliver, but judging by the expression on your faces four months isn't what you wanted to hear."

Daniel shifted uncomfortably, looking from one face to the next.

"We could have ten operations between now and then," Kaeden remarked.

"Or you could pace yourself until you're fully outfitted," Daniel countered.

Kae, Marcie, and Auburn started to laugh.

"You don't know Dad or the pack. The only reason we

won't have *twenty* ops is..." Kae stopped, pickled his expression, and turned to Marcie.

"There *is* no reason. Just travel, and since we can gate within a star's gravity well, even that doesn't take long. So ten, twenty-five—whatever it may be. You can guaran-damn-tee that we're going to be busy," Marcie explained.

"I'll do my best," Daniel told them. He couldn't guarantee anything except that he would make calls and try to instill the sense of urgency into his supply chain.

"I'll ask my dad to call Nathan and see if we can get a little extra horsepower on our side," Kae said, as if reading Daniel's mind.

After they looked at each other for a few moments they realized there was no more conversation left, so the warriors nodded politely and left.

"Dad is running the levels?" Kae asked once they were in the corridor.

"That's what I hear. I think he's got the pack with him, so you should be able to hear their grumbling before you see them."

"Why weren't we invited?" Kae liked the unit runs.

"Because we show up to work outs on time. The pack acts like they're back in New York City." Marcie listened, then looked up and down the corridor. Terry and the others would run through the one they were in at some point in their journey.

"How would *you* know what they were like back then?"

"I know this one!" Auburn interjected, waiting a few moments before delivering his punchline. "Because Char said they were acting that way."

They chuckled together until interrupted by a distant voice.

"Would you keep up?" Terry Henry Walton bellowed from well down the corridor. The station was round, but didn't need to rotate to maintain artificial gravity. The outer rings on each deck provided the longest routes.

Logistics was located between two docking bays for ease of transloading raw materials. The automated factory occupied the interior section of the deck. When major deliveries were being made, the corridor was closed as equipment moved back and forth from outer to inner areas. The next ship wasn't due for a week, so the space was open and free for recreational use.

Or torture, which TH appeared to be inflicting. He had picked up his pace to the inhuman speeds that the enhanced could achieve and Char was right behind him, but Dokken fell back. No one else was in sight.

Marcie was waiting at an intersection and held out a hand to stop the train heading down the tracks. Terry reared back as he pulled up and breathed deeply and quickly. Char matched his pose, hands on her head to expand her lungs more fully and pull in the most air possible. Dokken trotted up, tongue lolling.

I think you are a horrible human, Dokken broadcast to everyone's chip.

"What do you mean?" Terry replied defensively.

I don't run like that. If you wanted to see how fast you could go, you should have left me out of it. I'm done with this exercise in fertility.

"Futility," Terry corrected.

Exactly. Dokken limped away.

"Hang on, are you hurt?" Terry hurried to the dog's side, checking his rear leg. Dokken yipped when Terry touched a certain place.

He picked Dokken up gingerly and started to run. "We're going to the Pod-doc!" he yelled out the side of his mouth.

Dokken stuck his tongue out at the group of watchers, dog-smiling over Terry's shoulder.

Char watched them go. "I think my husband just got played by a German Shepherd. Let's follow in case there's fireworks."

Char took off after TH and the others fell in behind her.

Ted looked at Ankh, who returned his gaze. To someone who didn't know them they would have appeared to be in a staring contest, but they weren't.

They were linking through the artificial intelligence called "Plato" using the advanced chips that Ted had designed. So far only Ted and Ankh had had them surgically implanted in their brains.

Ted considered it liberating, as if his consciousness were expanding to fill the universe. He was in a place that challenged his mind all day, every day.

Ankh looked at problems in ways Ted would not have considered, and the insight from an alien mind made Ted better.

Ted appreciated Ankh, validation which he hadn't received from his fellow Crenellians. They went about their business and did their jobs, staying physically as far as possible from their fellows. Basically, they lived within their computer systems. The small alien had the best of all worlds with the Bad Company. He had access to more powerful computers than he had imagined existed, and he had the freedom to explore both the real and virtual worlds.

He'd even drunk a beer.

Ted blinked and glared at Ankh. "Beer? You should be thinking about interstellar communication. How do we burst the signal for instantaneous transfer?"

The Crenellian's big head bobbed about before he stood. "I apologize for my distraction. How long have we been at this?"

Ted glanced at the clock, but it was inconclusive. He needed more data. "What day is it?"

Plato said through the room's speakers, "You've been at this for more than two days, and you are both malnourished and dehydrated. You need to drink, eat, and rest—in that order, please. I will shut down all research and development systems for the next ten hours."

"You can't do that. We have work to do!" Ted stood too and looked from screen to screen, but they were all dark. "Plato?"

Ankh reached over his head to stretch, the skin tightening across his ribs. "Yes. Food would be a good idea."

Ted didn't want to leave. He thought they were ready to cross the next threshold; to be that much closer to a solution regarding instantaneous interstellar communications. Infinite power took care of a number of problems, which meant they could focus elsewhere and keep knocking down the obstacles until there weren't any more.

And he needed those communications so he and Felicity could talk with their kids to find out what was going on back on Earth. How were they holding up?

The others wanted to talk to those they had left had behind as well. The issue was always there, but no one discussed it. Ted was about to change that by opening a channel so everyone could stay in touch with their families.

After a meal and some sleep, of course.

Dokken came out of the Pod-doc much perkier than he had gone in. "Thank you," Terry told the technician running the advanced device. Char stood behind TH, shaking her head and holding a finger to her lips.

The technician nodded. "You're welcome."

Char smiled and mouthed the words, "thank you."

I feel like a new dog! Dokken exclaimed, twitching his eyebrows. *No more runs.*

"I thought you were a little more stalwart. No wonder you can't catch Wenceslaus! Is it just me, or have you noticed that the cat is getting fat?"

Dokken huffed, coughed, and barked. *Blasphemy! He has help, and you know it. That engineer is sheltering him, and I suspect Smedley Butler is in on it too.*

"You like Clodagh, and *you* know it."

Do not. She smells of cat. It makes me sneeze.

"I see. Maybe if you spent more time with her you'd block the Good King Wenceslaus. He would come to you."

You may have a point, human. I will consider it once we are back aboard the War Axe.

"Until then, dog, what's our next move?"

Dokken sat, rocked backwards, and used a back paw to scratch the side of his head. When he was finished he stood and shook himself, causing a small cloud of hair to rise into the air.

The technician sighed.

"We'll get out of your hair," Terry said, embracing the pun as he hurried from the medical space. Char and Dokken led the way out.

Once in the corridor, Dokken stopped and looked up at Terry Henry. *Thank you for taking care of me, but I must be off now. See you around dinnertime?*

"Where do you have to go?" Terry wondered aloud.

Places to go, people to see, Dokken replied as he trotted away.

"You know he wasn't really injured," Char said, watching the German Shepherd happily wagging his tail as he turned a corner and disappeared.

"I know. I told the technician to *not* do anything with the Pod-doc. He closed the door, turned on the lights for a minute, and opened the door. I was running poor Dokken into the ground, and carrying him here was my way of apologizing. He knows it and I know it, but as long as no one says it out loud we can hold on to our dignity."

Char snorted as she draped her arms around her husband's neck. "And what, if I may ask, is your definition of dignity?"

"'The summer's flow'r is to the summer sweet, Though to itself it only live and die, But if that flow'r with base infection meet, The basest weed outbraves his dignity. For sweetest things turn sourest by their deeds; Lilies that fester smell far worse than weeds,'" Terry quoted from Shakespeare.

"After you made Felicity cry you probably don't want to show your face on the promenade, my festering lily." Char's purple eyes sparkled and her hair perfectly framed her face, the silver streak trailing down one side.

"I am smitten," TH admitted.

"How about a shower? You're kind of rank."

"I'm all kinds of colonel, aren't I?"

Char pushed him away. "You promoted yourself once a hundred and thirty years ago. Your upward mobility sucks."

"Rank it is, my love." Terry took Char's hand as they started walking toward the quarters area of the station. "And then a staff meeting to refine the planning for Benitus Seven."

Char stopped. "You could have brought that up after dessert."

"Are we going to lunch?"

Char rolled her eyes and shook her head. "Last one to our place has to clean up the bathroom." She launched herself forward at werewolf speed, and it dawned on Terry what she'd been talking about.

Too worried about the next op to see what's right in front of you, he thought as he accelerated, enjoying the wind of his passing blowing his hair back. He smiled as he sprinted to keep Char in sight. She ran effortlessly.

This is why we do what we do. The freedom to be happy, so people can play without worry about whether they'll be alive tomorrow or not, whether that tear in the dimensional fabric will affect them. Monsters! It is our job to give the people the joy of ignorance. No one needs to know the danger, only that the Bad Company will protect them.

CHAPTER THREE

"We don't know a whole lot, do we?" Marcie stated after the initial briefing.

Terry Henry Walton shook his head. "This meeting is about filling in the gaps in our knowledge. We've built a recon plan. Kaeden?"

"You bet, Pops," Kae replied, standing up.

Terry stopped him. "'Pops?' Where the hell did you get that from?"

"Some old black and white movies. It sounded groovy." Kae nodded to the others in the room—werewolves, weretigers, vampires, aliens, and those in Terry and Char's family, enhanced by nanocytes and leaders all.

Terry turned to Char and whispered, "I'm not sure I like that."

Char shushed him.

"Returning to the matter at hand…" Kae began. He was nearly one hundred and fifty years old, but embraced the youth that the nanocytes gave his body. Regardless of appearance, Kaeden was a skilled tactician and experienced in combat.

"As you've taught us, there is nothing like having eyes on target before committing to a final action plan. Let's talk about what that looks like…"

Felicity leaned back in her overstuffed chair behind her oversized desk. Daniel stood in front of the desk with a man dressed like a prison inmate. An armed security guard stood behind the pair.

"I'd like to introduce Brice. He's one of the few who isn't incapacitated by the sight of a woman."

"Good morning, Brice." Felicity knew why they were there, but wanted to wait until the man spoke.

"Good morning, ma'am," he said in a soft voice, looking at the desktop. "My name is 'Bo-ah-Rice,' but I like the way you pronounce it."

Daniel looked surprised.

"'Brice' it is. What can I help you with?"

"We are eating the rations from our ships, but those will run out soon. We will need food if we are to survive, but as our captors, it is yours to decide if we live or die."

Felicity smiled pleasantly, draping her blonde hair behind one ear. "That's not how we do business. You were freed from your oppression by the Direct Action Branch, but you are now under my protection and I'm the senior civilian authority in these parts. Your lives are not in jeopardy," Felicity drawled slowly as he leaned forward on her desk.

"The food?" the man asked.

"Already ordered. A freighter should arrive within the next few days. They will also be carrying a great stock of spacesuits. We need your people to help us build a functioning shipyard where we can repair or upgrade any vessel which visits. That work is very important to us, and every worker will be paid in Federation credits. The workforce will have quarters on this station with access to all that we have here—restaurants, shops, recreation, people."

"How will the females be apportioned? Surely there aren't enough to go around?"

"I'm sorry. I saw your lips moving and heard some words come out, but none of them made any sense to me," Felicity replied in a low and dangerous voice.

The man stuttered, but stopped before he said anything else.

"From what I hear, the entity known as 'Ten' picked a select few for breeding, and they remained behind on Home World. Everyone else was put to work and prevented from interacting with women in any way," Daniel offered.

"This is the truth," Brice confirmed.

"Holy shit." Felicity covered her mouth with one hand at her verbal transgression. "I've been around those vagrants and mongrels for too long..." Felicity shook her head and sighed before continuing, "What was that? You don't ever get to see women?"

"The first women we have seen have been those from the Bad Company. You are the first woman I've ever talked to. May I touch your hair?"

"No. You may not touch my hair. We need someone to

train eleven hundred men in how to treat women, appropriate social skills…" Felicity's eyes crossed as she pondered the inconceivable. "I have it—it has to be me."

Daniel shifted his weight from one foot to the other, and the guard looked nervous.

"What's your name back there?" Felicity asked.

The guard pointed to himself, and Felicity nodded.

"There are those who call me 'Tim,'" he replied ominously.

"As long as one of those was your mother I'll accept that. Tim, I'm going to make you my liaison to our guests. He's not to touch my hair or any other part of me or any other woman on this station. Then we'll need to set up a way to talk with these people. By the way, what do you call yourselves?"

Brice wore a blank expression.

"Hello?" Felicity stared at the man.

"Nothing," he finally replied.

"That won't do. How should we identify you? Because we surely are not going to call you 'the captives.' You are free to become contributing members of our society. The only choice you *won't* have is to return to the fold on Home World. I suspect that once Terry Henry and his gang get done with it, there won't be anything to go back to anyway."

All three men stood uncomfortably before Felicity's desk.

"Fine. Tim, take Brice for a walk around the station. Introduce him to some people, like the shipyard manager and as many of the foremen as you can find. Let's see how we can temper our approach and bring an army of good workers on board."

Tim nodded politely and ushered Brice out. Daniel waited. Felicity rolled her finger at him. *Out with it.*

"If we don't get a resupply on food within the next couple days we'll have to start rationing." His forehead wrinkled in concern.

"I know, Daniel, but the first one should arrive in time and deliver enough to get us by until our big shipments hit. With this kind of manpower we might have to get our own gate, because the freighters are limited to traveling with the big warships. My husband is working on something so even little ships will be able to gate. That could solve our problems, and these are some big problems," Felicity drawled.

"Isn't Keeg Station supposed to be a secret, and that's why there's no gate? If all the freighters can make their own gates and have our coordinates, we won't be much of a secret." Daniel didn't have an answer. He only saw problems for the foreseeable future.

"When you have a big dance people will come, no matter whether they're invited or not. I'll talk to our benefactor in the Bad Company and see what we can do."

Daniel frowned and nodded. "I can't give them the armor they need and we can't feed them. We're not much of a support team."

He started to walk out of the office.

"We're doing better than that," she replied. "We're doing everything we've been asked to do, and then some. They've more than doubled our manpower. We need more space as well as more supplies, and they *are* sending us more. We are doing okay, and the sky is the limit for Keeg Station."

Daniel didn't stop walking. He understood that it meant more work for everyone, and more work wasn't necessarily good.

Felicity keyed her comm system. "Sue, can you come to my office? There's an administrative problem that I need your help with. And if you have that delightful hunk of man candy with you, bring him, too."

The Director of Keeg Station leaned back in her comfortable chair, steepled her fingers before her, and tried to think through the logistics problems that would soon plague her station. She closed her eyes and whispered a prayer for relief before anyone else realized the coming stampede of issues.

"Ted. We need drones that we can drop within the atmosphere to conduct aerial reconnaissance. Do the the reconnaissance, the recce so we don't put anyone at unnecessary risk," Terry explained as he took care not to touch anything in Ted's laboratory.

"I'm working on something. Come back later." Ted turned away, but Terry moved until he was in Ted's way.

"There is no later, Ted. We're embarking soon, and you're coming with us."

"I have work to do *here*," Ted replied matter-of-factly.

"'Miniaturized Etheric power source.' Does that ring a bell? We need you to evaluate it and then download the technology, including any raw materials we might need that are unique to Benitus Seven."

Ted's eyes unfocused, and Terry took that as a sign that Ted was contemplating what he could do with such an engineering marvel. When Ted blinked, he moved to his bench and started tinkering.

"Well?" TH asked.

"Well what?" Ted replied.

"Pack your trash. We're going aboard the *War Axe*," Terry declared.

"Why?" Ted stopped tinkering and looked skeptically at the colonel.

"Because we can't get to Benitus without taking the ship."

"Why would I need to go to Benitus? Go beat up those devil things and then bring the Beniton technology back here. It's not that hard. I thought you were smarter. Space has made you dumb."

Terry threw his head back and stared at the ceiling with a stunned mullet expression, then exhaled loudly.

He clenched his fists as he tried to get it across. "Ted. You're going with us. Period. Bring Plato and your toys. I will send a squad from Kim's platoon to carry you and your stuff to the shuttle. You have one hour."

"But I'm not going."

"Ted!" Terry leaned forward, ready to scream in frustration. "Did you not hear anything I've said the past fifteen minutes?"

"Not really. I think I've solved a transceiver integration problem. See? Look at this…"

Terry walked away.

"In one hour, you will be on that shuttle. Conscious or unconscious is your choice. You can run, but you can't hide."

Terry stopped and accessed his comm chip. *Kimber, can you detail a few of your people to help Ted get ready for our next deployment?*

I anticipated as much so I had one squad report early. They'll be on their way momentarily from the hangar bay.

He thinks he's not going, so tell them to ignore anything he says. They should carry him if they have to.

I get you—Ted is coming no matter what. Do you think it would help if I came along?

I didn't want to ask, but since it sounds like you're offering I think it would help a great deal. Get your Uncle Ted on board. Terry sighed in relief. He looked over his shoulder to find Ted completely embroiled within a holographic projection. Where was that Crenellian?

Fitzroy can handle the platoon. I'm on my way, Kimber replied.

And bring Ankh, if you can find him.

Sheri's Pride, Alien Ship of the Line in Orbit around Keeg Station

"Everyone settle down!" one of the guards called. He had been working as a maintenance technician, but given the massive number of prisoners, he had been conscripted to work security on the captured ship. As long as the guards were all men, the human captives weren't a problem.

They had tried two female guards, but there was nearly

a riot. A third of the men wanted to throw the women out the airlock, but the other two-thirds would have worshipped them as goddesses had Marcie Walton allowed it. She was in charge, but Kaeden's was the official face of the Bad Company on the *Sheri's Pride* even though he wasn't aboard the ship. When they needed to speak to the captives, they transmitted to the screens that filled the largest space on the warship.

All the captives would gather to watch, and following the briefings they would go about the mundane duties Plato assigned them. They each had their duty pad in a cargo pocket or their hand. The men from Home World never went anywhere without them.

The screens came to life, and a blue-eyed blonde woman appeared. She smiled pleasantly, and looked from left to right as if she were looking at the crowd. In a way, she was. Their image was projected to her screen just as hers was projected to theirs.

A couple of the men started yelling, but others encouraged them to shut up. There was a bit of a scrum before things settled down.

"My name is Felicity, and I'm the Director of Keeg Station. Today I'll be giving you your first lesson in etiquette. That is, how to assimilate into a culture with women, not just by your side, doing the same job you're doing, but maybe in charge of you. How will you deal with that?"

Felicity smiled and watched the men, who were sitting silently.

They couldn't see her clenching her fists off-screen

"Since none of you seem to have the answer, I'll give it

to you: you treat them no differently. They are professionals with jobs to do, just like you, just like I'm doing now," she drawled. She didn't think her words were registering. "I know we may look different…"

Felicity let the pause drag out as she focused her eyes like lasers. Each man thought she was looking at him.

"Do you like my hair? No blonde hair where you come from? Do you want to touch it? Well, *you can't!*" Felicity glared from the monitors on *Sheri's Pride* for a moment, then straightened her clothes and leaned back. Her smile returned. "And that, gentlemen, is your lesson for today. I'll be back tomorrow with more of the same."

The screen went dark, and the men sat there. The guards let them remain in place until the murmuring started.

"*Check your pads for your orders!*" one of the guards yelled.

Almost as one, the men pulled out their pads and the screens came to life. Once they saw their tasks, they got up and headed out.

The guard's comm system came to life. "Yes, sir," the man replied, seeing that it was Kaeden.

"What is your feeling on how they received their first lesson?" Kae asked without preamble.

"I don't know. They weren't too responsive, but they live for their pads. Once they were told to check their maintenance orders they were instantly engaged."

"Thanks for the insight. Kaeden out."

CHAPTER FOUR

Keeg Station

"Nicely done, Felicity," Sue told the station director. Timmons leaned against the wall with his arms crossed. He pursed his lips, sucked them in, and pursed them a second time.

Kaeden stood with his back to them as he looked out the window.

"Stoic. That's how I'd describe them," Kae muttered.

"But the guard said that they responded to their pads." Sue joined Kae at the window. In the distance, they could see *Sheri's Pride* along with the other ships that had been captured during the Alchon mission.

"I may have to go over there in person," Felicity drawled.

"No, you don't," Sue cautioned, turning to look at the director. "You really don't. Not until they're housebroken, at the very least."

Kae chuckled to himself.

"Remember way back when cell phones were the rage?

If we can push messages to the pads until they are used to seeing women, it might be easier when they actually *see* women. We'll play videos on how men should treat women. These guys can learn by watching others," Timmons offered.

"Who is going to make the videos?" Sue asked skeptically.

"No one. We'll let Smedley or Plato pick them."

"This station needs its own AI. We can't always count on Smedley being here or Plato being available. My dear husband won't like us volunteering his new girlfriend, Plato." Felicity got up and joined the others at the window.

Timmons continued to lean against the wall as he looked at the ceiling in concentration.

"Smedley's only an EI, but he's pretty smart," Kae said.

"Smedley is as much an EI as you or me," Timmons countered. "No, we need their help. I guess you better get a request to the Federation for an AI. Why wasn't there one here before we arrived?"

"No need, and then when you got here Smedley filled in. Then *we* got here and Ted is Ted, so he turned Plato loose on my unsuspecting station."

The comm unit buzzed on Felicity's desk, and she reached back and grabbed it. "Speak of the devil," she said before answering it. "It's my husband. I don't know if you've ever called me in the middle of the day before."

"They're making me go, and I don't want to," Ted complained.

Kae snorted at the window before covering his mouth and laughing into his hand. Sue slowly shook her head, and Timmons continued to stare at the ceiling.

"I think it's best you go, my dear. I'd love to come along, but integrating these new workers is taking far more effort than I had planned." Felicity gave the others a thumbs-up.

"But I don't *want* to go. I want to talk with our kids. I'm close, Felicity—close to having a working model. Then someone will need to take the other transceivers to Earth…once we have the miniaturized Etheric power supplies, of course, but that's a given. I just need to have everything ready for when they arrive."

"If you go along, you can work on the integration while TH and his people are clearing out those vile horned creatures. You'll be able to finish sooner than if you waited here. You must go! *I want to talk with our children.*"

There was a long delay before Ted spoke again. "Okay."

"One other thing, my husband. We need an AI for the station. Do you have one lying around?"

"AIs don't lie around, Felicity, but Plato has stepchildren. Activate your access link and say, 'I need you, Dionysus,' then say the names and birthdates of our children followed by the date of our marriage. Plato's stepchildren are already within the system, and Dionysus is ready to serve. Leave the others where they are, please. I have a different task for them."

Kae's jaw fell and he looked at the comm device in disbelief.

A single tear streamed down Felicity's cheek. "I can't wait for you to get home from your latest adventure, my love." Felicity choked and could say no more.

"Terry Henry Walton better not get me killed." Ted clicked off. Felicity sobered instantly and glared at Kaeden.

"You keep my husband safe!" she ordered. "And while you're at it, you keep my daughter safe, too."

Kaeden hugged his mother-in-law. "Always. Well, as much as she'll let me. I don't see Ted going landside on Benitus Seven. He should be able to remain in his laboratory with Plato on the ship for the duration, doing Ted stuff."

Felicity held Kae for a few seconds longer. "I guess that means you will be leaving soon."

"Right now, as a matter of fact. Good luck training your boys," Kae told her. Kae looked at Sue. "Coming?"

Sue shook her head. "Timmons and I need to stay behind. There is so much to do with the shipyard! We need an engineer and another manager if we want to have any hope of integrating those people into our society, and more importantly into our workforce."

"Does the colonel know?" Kae asked as he headed for the door.

"Not yet."

"You know how he likes surprises!" Kae walked briskly through the door on his way to the hangar bay.

Felicity returned to her chair. "Well?"

"Well what?" Sue replied.

"Call TH and get it over with. Turn on the waterworks, and he'll melt. He's a quintessential man, so we can't ever have him teach any of the classes to help this bunch social-ize." Felicity pointed at the window.

"Is that what we're going to call them? Everything with them is so vanilla, but they are creepy in person. A whole colony of creepy guys. Don't ever ask me to go to that ship. I've been on one of them already, and that was plenty."

"I'll second that," Timmons said. He pushed away from the wall and strolled to a nearby chair, which he flopped into.

"You're the senior werewolf. Maybe *you* should call TH and tell him."

With raised eyebrows, Timmons looked at his mate. "I like Felicity's approach."

"Chicken." She looked around the room, twisted her mouth sideways, and shook her head. "Fine."

Felicity handed the comm over.

"TH, are you there?" Sue asked pleasantly, grinning as if trying to pass a kidney stone.

"We're all here. Where are you?" Terry replied impatiently.

"We have to stay behind to help Felicity with this mob we brought back from Alchon Prime. You don't need us on this one, do you?"

"Get your fucking asses down here right fucking now!" Terry bellowed into the comm.

Timmons nodded, gave them a thumbs-up, and rolled a finger for Sue to continue. She shook her head, and he smiled and kept rolling his finger.

"Integrating this workforce is going to take a great deal of effort...far more than Felicity can do by herself," Sue patiently explained.

In the background, they heard Marcie's voice. "No kidding, TH! Mom's starting to get crow's feet around her eyes."

"I heard that!" Felicity immediately put a finger to the corner of her eye to try to feel the cracks.

Scratching, and then muffled speech. Sue and Timmons looked at each other.

"Fine," Terry declared. "By 'we' I expect you mean Timmons, too."

Timmons stood up straight and rolled his hands palm upward. *What the hell?*

"Yes. We have a lot of work to do if we're to build a functioning shipyard capable of repairing the damage that you have an innate ability to cause to our ship. It'll be no picnic back here. We'd rather be with you." Sue winked at Timmons.

"Of course you would. I said 'Fine' and I meant "Fine." We will see you when we get back, and you'd better have a fully functioning shipyard since you know we're going to limp in here twelve different kinds of broken."

"If you don't return for six months we might be there. In a week? We'll see what we can have ready," Sue countered.

Terry's device clicked twice and went silent.

"He sounded pretty mad," Timmons suggested. Sue nodded. "When does rationing start?"

Felicity looked at her desk and then out the window. "Tomorrow," she replied softly.

"Sounds like we're going out for lunch today!" Timmons crooked his arm and Sue took it as the two danced out the door.

Felicity watched them go, unsure what had been accomplished. She got up, paced back and forth a few times, and then stopped at the window. Six shuttles launched from the hangar bay and made a lazy turn as they headed toward the *War Axe*.

"Activate voice command, please," she told her computer. "I need you, Dionysus."

Terry wore a sour expression as Char laughed softly beside him.

"It's not funny. They're hanging us out to dry."

"By working for the long term? Felicity can't do it all, especially when you keep adding new recruits to the mix. We have sixteen suits of powered armor against a techno-logically-inferior enemy. What are you worried about?" Char asked.

"It seems like we're relying on the mechs to do all the work."

"So? And what does that have to do with Timmons and Sue sitting this one out? We ordered suits for everyone because the meat-sack versions of the warriors are vulner-able, even with being enhanced. We will have a hard time no matter where we go if we're not suited up, so the mechs make sense. We'll keep leaning heavily on the ones we have until everyone has one. It's just perception, TH. We still need to use our heads in combat—there's no substitute for that."

"Wise beyond your years, my lover," Terry replied.

Char leaned away from her husband. "Are you saying I'm old?"

Terry saw that he had been painted into a corner. Words had been put into his mouth. There was no escape, but it wasn't checkmate.

"You're my hot young babe. If you ever get old, let me know so I can trade you in on a new model."

Char elbowed Terry in the ribs. "Nice try, and there will be no trading in, up, down, or any which way but loose."

"Nice orangutan reference. Well done." TH managed to smile.

The shuttle slowed and entered *War Axe's* hangar bay, where it maneuvered into position to be reloaded into the drop tube.

Terry watched the shuttle's front screen, where the external camera showed a supply of ballistic canisters secured in a corner. "Who ordered the cans?" Terry asked.

"Probably Auburn," Marcie replied from the other side of the shuttle Pod.

"Sounds like a good standard operating procedure item. Planetside operations, be prepared to resupply." *SOP.* Terry nodded to himself as the shuttle settled in and the rear hatch opened.

Terry and Char waited for the others to disembark—Marcie, Joseph, Petricia, Christina, Bundin, Cory, Ramses, and Dokken. Actually, no one had to wait for the German Shepherd because he was the first out, vaulting over the ramp to hit the deck. He kept running and someone opened the hatch for him and he was through, speeding into the bowels of the ship.

Smedley, we're back. Make sure everyone knows that Dokken is hunting the Good King. I think his doghood was questioned when we were on the station, and he may be trying to prove himself, Terry told General Smedley Butler.

I shall make the appropriate notifications. We can't have Wenceslaus get trapped in a corner somewhere. And welcome back, my friends! It will be so nice to start a new adventure with you, the EI replied.

Char watched Terry commune with the ship's integrated and evolved intelligence. Terry was a genius in many ways, but walking and using the comm chip at the same time was not one of them. Whenever he talked with anyone using the comm chip embedded in his brain, it took his full concentration.

Are you an AI now? Terry asked.

I am completing my final papers as part of the AI extension course that ArchAngel devised. Night school has been fabulous for me, I must admit. You should sit in on one of the sessions if you can. You do speak binary, don't you? No matter...I hope to have my certification and tassel soon.

Terry snorted. *You have me confused with Ted. No, I don't speak binary. Are you pulling my leg? It sure sounds like you're yanking my chain. A certification for evolution? Dammit, Smedley, I wish I could tell if you're joking or not. Let the captain know that we're on our way to the bridge, if you would be so kind.*

I always try to be kind. I will let you know when I have sufficiently evolved to appropriately wear the title of AI.

Eat me, Terry replied, before blinking himself back into the real world. Char had waited patiently on the edge of the ramp while he stood there by himself.

Everyone else was gone, leaving the hangar bay empty.

"Must have been some conversation," Char told him as they took each other's hand and walked away from the drop ship.

"Smedley is giving me some bunk about not being an AI until he gets a certificate from night school. That's just bullsh… That's rubbish." Terry caught himself in time, and grinned at Char.

"I'm proud of you," she said in a motherly tone.

He smirked and looked away. "The habits we pick up over time. A trap, so easy to fall into. Like you…why are you physically incapable of hanging your towel on the rack when you're done with it?"

Charumati shrugged. "Maybe I like seeing you bend over to pick it up."

"I don't think that's it."

They continued through the hatch and headed for the stairwell that led to the bridge.

"Maybe it's because I just don't care if it's on the rack or not."

"I think you're getting closer. You know I'll pick it up, and I think you like using a dry towel, so this is about me and not your towel."

"It's the price you have to pay to see me naked."

"The price of freedom?" Terry waited until they were on the stairs, then faced upward, cupped a hand around his mouth, and yelled, "FREEDOM!"

"What did I get myself into?"

"An adventure worthy of Klingon opera," Terry said without hesitation. "For a hundred and thirty-some years I've paid the price to see you naked, and I don't regret a single minute of it."

Char pulled him to a stop and wrapped her arms around his head as she pulled him close for a long kiss. His hand found its way under her shirt to caress the skin of her back.

"MY GOD!" Kaeden yelled. "My eyes, they burn."

Terry jumped sideways, expecting danger. He and Char had been behind the others, but they had gone to their quarters first. Now, Terry and Char were ahead as they mobbed the stairwell from the deck where they were billeted. Family and friends, werewolves, weretigers, vampires, and aliens. There was no threat, only judgmental looks. He relaxed and smiled.

"Why are you sneaking around?" Terry wondered.

"No sneaking here," Kimber replied.

"Yes, there is no sneaking," Bundin said from farther down the stairwell.

"Did you hear them?" Terry looked confused.

"Yes. I didn't care to do anything about it, though. I preferred what I was doing at the moment."

"Well, yeah, me too, but I should have heard something." Terry looked up the stairway. When he turned back, he wore a strange expression. He pointed ahead using a hatchet motion with his arm. "Wagons...*HO!*"

He stomped up the stairs.

"It's been a while since we've heard that one," Shonna grumbled. "He did that every time we left camp on the big move from New Boulder to North Chicago. Every. Single. Time."

CHAPTER FIVE

Ted and Ankh stood side by side, looking at the laboratory.

"I suggest we continue with the communications system. We are so close I can taste it," the Crenellian suggested.

"I've seen you eat. I don't understand how you can taste anything." Ted set down the box containing Plato. Even though it had a small integrated power supply, he used the wireless power throughout the *War Axe* when possible to extend the life of Plato's internal source. But there were backups to backups. Even if he ran out of power, Plato would continue to exist. The only limitation would be to Plato's interaction with the outside world. "Plato, what do you suggest we work on?"

We were making such incredible progress on the interstellar communications unit that I don't want to stop.

"The 'I See You,'" Ankh enunciated.

"I agree. That is what we should be working on."

What else do we have? Ankh asked, switching to his comm chip.

We have the power source for the armored suits, energy shields for the warriors, cloaking technology, and mini-gate technology to start with, Ted recited.

I think you shall kill three birds with one stone when you obtain the miniaturized Etheric power supply from the Benitons, Plato replied.

Interstellar communications it was. Ted stepped onto the pad and surrounded himself with a holo image of the interior circuitry. Ankh assumed his position on a secondary pad and activated its holo screens.

Soon, the two were embroiled within a digital web, happy in their own ways as they disappeared into their virtual world.

"Clodagh, please keep a close eye on Wenceslaus. From what I hear, Dokken has had his doghood challenged and now he's 'on the warpath,' if I got the human colloquialism correct," Smedley said.

"Had his doghood challenged?" Clodagh Shortall repeated. "I don't know what that means, but the Good King is right here. Wait a minute. Where'd you go, little guy? Danger! I have lost the Good King. All hands on deck!"

Clodagh laughed to herself as she resumed working at her station.

"I don't think you're taking this seriously." Smedley tried to sound put out.

"I think Wenceslaus can take care of himself. He was

dodging dogs long before you or I started giving him a hand. He's his own cat."

Through the open hatch echoed the furious barking of a German Shepherd engaged in mortal combat.

"Dammit!" Clodagh yelled as she bolted from the space.

"Hang on!" Commander Suresha called after her, but it was too late. The lieutenant ran down the corridor toward the sound of a dog barking.

Clodagh raced toward the sound. "Gangway!" she yelled, to avoid colliding with two maintenance techs working on a lower side hatch. They ducked as she vaulted over them.

She sped up when she heard a cat's snarl and a long, low growl. Clodagh banked off a bulkhead to change direction into a side passage.

Dokken had the orange cat cornered between two closed hatches at the end of a short corridor.

"LEAVE HIM ALONE!" the human screamed, and hit the deck as if she were sliding into second base. In one smooth motion, she pushed Dokken aside as she passed him and deftly scooped Wenceslaus into her arms before coming back to her feet.

One more bark, then Dokken cocked his head sideways.

"Shame on you! As an evolved creature, it is disgraceful that you pick on a defenseless kitten."

He is my arch enemy, Dokken declared weakly. *Look what he did to my nose!*

Clodagh turned to keep her body between the dog and the cat held tightly in her arms and peered down on Dokken's snout.

Wenceslaus dug two paws' worth of claws into her arm and she jumped, but didn't lose her grip. "And you stop it!"

A single drop of blood dripped from the slice across the top of Dokken's nose.

"Good. Serves you right for sticking that thing where it doesn't belong." The cat continued to squirm. "Wenceslaus! I'm going to feed you to the dog if you don't settle down."

When the Good King raked a sharp, long claw down her arm she gave up trying to hold him, and he dropped to the deck. Dokken barked once, but stopped when Clodagh shook her finger at him.

Pounding footsteps signaled the arrival of reinforcements. Terry Henry Walton was first to appear, followed closely by Aaron and Yanmei.

"My arch nemesis! Aha, we've got you now," Terry declared, shaking a fist.

Aaron leaned over the dog and Wenceslaus launched himself upward. Dokken snapped at empty air as the weretiger caught the Good King and hefted him well out of reach. Without a word, Aaron and Yanmei walked away, the orange cat cradled between them.

"You let our arch nemesis get away," Terry said sadly.

Look what he did to my nose. Dokken lifted his head and Terry leaned down. They met halfway.

"That's going to leave a cool scar." Terry vigorously scratched behind the German Shepherd's ear. "What do you say we go see Jenelope and snag some bistok jerky? It's not bacon, but it's the closest we're going to get out here."

"What about the meeting?" Smedley asked over the ship-wide broadcast.

"But first, my furry friend, back to the captain's conference room."

Terry tried to look nonchalant as he followed Aaron and Yanmei down the corridor with Dokken in tow.

When Terry arrived at the conference room, Wenceslaus was sprawled in the middle of the table. No one spoke but everyone waited for TH's reaction. He swept his gaze past the cat as if it were a common occurrence. Dokken sniffed the tabletop, then worked his way around, letting everyone scratch his ears and pet his head.

Even Aaron and Yanmei petted the German Shepherd.

You smell like cat.

"It's the bane of our existence," Aaron replied. The weretigers chuckled at the dog's observation.

The room smelled of sandalwood rather than the musk of sweaty bodies. Two drawings had been added to the walls since Terry had last been here. Both were alien landscapes which at one time would have been fantastic, but as humanity had expanded through space the fantastic had become commonplace.

All the chairs were taken, leaving many people to stand. Christina leaned against a wall with her arms crossed, and Bundin was wedged into the corner. The Podder took up too much space to stand anywhere else. The Crenellian and Ted weren't there.

Captain Micky San Marino watched the proceedings patiently. He was there because Terry and Char had asked him to be. Micky was as much an observer as the rest of those present.

"Smedley, bring up a holo of Benitus Seven," TH requested. The planet appeared and rotated slowly above the table. It was mostly green, comprised of eighty percent land and twenty percent water. The equator was arid and scorched, while the habitable zones ranged north and south from the desert belt. The poles were cool, but not frozen.

Terry pointed at the equator. "Red and hornies are coming through the interdimensional portal somewhere in there—right in the middle of the hot zone."

"Benitus has a hell, and the devils found their way to it," Char said.

"Looks like." Terry nodded and turned to Marcie. "Assets?"

"Firepower," Marcie said, nodding to her husband.

Kae stood. "Sixteen fully operational suits formed into four combat teams. No other heavy firepower. The enemy has no mechanical assets."

Terry pointed to himself.

"The only one in here who will get a suit is me." Kae pointed at Marcie. "According to the colonel you—" Kae waved his arm to indicate the rest of the room. "have separate missions, but the mechs will handle the heavy lifting. There is no doubt about that."

Terry's face fell as Kae sat down and Char leaned close.

"You knew you weren't getting one. You'll be the last to get one, by your own order," she whispered.

"Why would I give such a stupid order?" TH whispered back.

Char raised one eyebrow. "We have to fight the war. You need to let the others fight the battles."

"Sounds like someone smart said that," Terry replied, knowing that was what he'd told her earlier in the week.

"Something like that." Char's purple eyes sparkled before she returned her attention to the spinning globe.

"Logistics?" Marcie continued.

Auburn didn't stand, but pulled a pad from his pocket that looked similar to those the captives from the Alchon mission used.

"We are pre-loading a number of ballistic cans right now. I'm going to increase the amount of water we send down with you, and the amount in the resupply. What are the temperatures in the hot zone?"

"Hell. As hot as the Wastelands back on Earth. Daytime temps up to one hundred forty degrees Fahrenheit, sixty degrees Celsius."

The Weres cringed. Their nanocytes kept their body temperatures high, so they couldn't function as well in the heat. Char blew out a long breath. "You may want to rethink who gets suits and where we'll deploy."

Christina winced and her forehead creased as she considered working in the extreme heat. She didn't know how her were body would respond.

Terry stood and started to pace, weaving between his family and friends. "First and foremost, we have to stop more of the creatures—the aliens, the devils, whatever we want to call them—from coming through the interdimensional portal." Terry stopped and shook his head. "I never imagined saying those words. We're in space, fighting for universal peace. We're preparing to fight the devil himself, it looks like. And you know what?"

The group was used to Terry's speeches, but they listened intently because the words kept them grounded. No fortune and no glory.

"We're going to deliver humanity's single greatest export—a healthy dose of justice. You don't come to our dimension and start wreaking havoc. Fark these guys!" Terry looked down at the table.

"Fark?" Joseph asked.

Terry shrugged. "Give me some credit for trying," he mumbled.

Ramses shook his head as he started scribbling in his notepad. He stopped for a moment, shook his pen at TH, and went back to writing.

Terry stood up straight and resumed the planning session. "We're going to close the portal first, then it becomes a search-and-destroy mission. All hands will engage in the primary mission before we break into teams to go after them one by one."

"What if they surrender?" Joseph asked.

"A good question, Joseph. I don't see it, but as General Dwight D. Eisenhower said, 'In preparing for battle I have always found that plans are useless, but planning is indispensable.' We will plan, but flex when the time comes."

"We can bring them to a central location as prisoners," Marcie suggested. She sat twiddling her thumbs with her fingers laced as she thought through the issue. "We'll put them at our landing site, wherever that may be, then hopefully we can hand them off to the Benitons. The last thing I want to do is hop a shuttle with a devil on board."

"I can't stop hearing the song *Highway to Hell*," Terry said as he bobbed his head to the music playing in his mind.

"I thought it was just me," Char confided out of the corner of her mouth.

"Dokken, you're going with us." Terry's face turned serious. "We may need your tracking expertise to hunt down the devils if they scatter and run."

The German Shepherd contemplated the order. *When do I get my spacesuit?*

Terry turned to Auburn.

"What?" the man asked.

"Oh, sorry. You didn't hear. Dokken asked when his spacesuit was going to be ready," Terry clarified.

Auburn double-checked his pad before meeting Terry's gaze. "Probably not before this mission is over. Sorry."

"We'll make do. Next time we have to operate in space, buddy, you'll be there with us. Can you operate a jetpack?"

Dokken turned his head sideways before flopping to the floor, putting his head between his paws, and looking up with droopy eyes. Terry had to pace the other way so he didn't step on the dog.

He hesitated. "Sometimes you just have to stop and revel in the absurdity of it all." The others eyed TH. They all had the same question, and he answered it before anyone asked. "Don't step on the dog, who's intelligent and miffed because his spacesuit won't be ready for this mission—a mission where we have to fly a bazillion light years through space to remove and eliminate horned red-skinned devils from the very flames of hell. That's all we have to do, and it's not absurd at all."

Sixteen warriors tensed within their powered and armored suits as the hangar bay door opened. They activated the magnetic clamps on their boots before the artificial gravity was turned off.

"Capples, Kelly, and Praeter, take your squads outside and execute the training maneuvers. My squad, standby," Kae ordered.

The squad leaders affirmed the order.

"Second Mech Squad, portside egress. Follow my lead." Capples unlocked his boots and floated into the air, and with deft use of his jets he slowly maneuvered toward open space. His three warriors took off and arranged themselves into a diamond formation behind their squad leader. One left, one right, and one bringing up the rear directly behind the leader.

"Capples' Commandos are underway," Kae reported as the first group departed. "Next up, Kelly's Heroes."

Kae had been engrossed in watching old television programming that the new technology made available. New to him, old to others, but still fresh.

He'd fallen in love with Heinlein's *Starship Troopers*, but had only watched the movie. TH had gasped when he had heard that, and told Kae to read the book. Kae hadn't; he had opted to watch the animated series instead. Rico's Roughnecks resonated.

So he had given each of the mech squads a name that would remain as long as the squad leader was in place. The squad's legacy was tied to the person in charge. If they moved up and someone else took over, the legacy would start fresh.

Kelly jumped into the air to kickstart her jets, but she almost lost control as the suit rocketed toward the hangar's ceiling. She tucked, rolled, and landed feet-first, then flexed her knees and pushed off, using her jets to swoop past the other mechs. Her team joined her and the four raced out of the hangar bay, making a wide arc and disappearing to the ship's starboard side.

"Praeter's Predators: let's see what you got!" Kae called, bad grammar and all.

"Predators, on my mark. Three. Two. One." Together they slowly rose into the air, rotated as one, and accelerated toward the black maw of space. As they moved, they spread apart like the petals of a blossoming flower.

"Very nice, Corporal Praeter. You other meatheads need to see how it's supposed to be done, so watch this!"

Three squads chuckled together.

"Come on, Knights, our turn." Kae held up a hand, counting down with his fingers. The mechs unclamped and drifted upward, rotated horizontal to the deck, and slowly maneuvered from the hangar bay. Kaeden watched the icons representing the three other warriors of his squad on his heads-up display. They fell in behind him in diamond formation and raced into open space.

"I'm not sure I like the name, boss. Your name, sure, but Kae's Knights doesn't have a ring to it," Gomez said.

"I know what you mean. Kae's Killers? Kae-Cophony? Kae's Crushers?"

"What the hell does Kae-Cophony mean?"

"Cacophony. Discordance of sound. Disruption."

"Now I get it, but will anyone else?" Gomez pressed.

"Damn! You're a hard man, Gomez, but *I like it.* Disruption, as in tearing up the enemy without being labeled as killers. Poddern soured me on that one."

Gomez, at Kae's six o'clock—the rear position of the diamond formation—didn't answer. They'd swept downward and were racing along the *War Axe's* keel. The newly labeled Kae-Cophony was about to get busy.

"First stop, the rear engine housing for mock explosives placement," Kae recited the training mission's parameters. He was in charge, but each team had its own mission and operated independently. For Kae to reassert control over the other teams, something would have to go wrong or the squads needed to coalesce to mass firepower.

Something they could have used on Poddern. Fleeter still wasn't right, although all her limbs and faculties were intact. She was on board the *War Axe* at her request, but wasn't required to participate in anything except her sessions with the ship's therapist—who also happened to be the head chef.

Jenelope was sometimes handed people who had trouble of one type or another. She'd put them to work in the kitchen, and they'd talk. No one knew if Jenelope had a degree in therapy, and no one cared. She was effective.

I hope it works out, Fleeter. We want you back in the ranks, Kae thought as his team slowed their approach to the massive engine housings at the *War Axe's* stern. He shook off his reverie and focused on the task at hand, knowing that both his father and wife were watching all four teams conduct the training missions.

The Colonels Walton. He laughed to himself. *Why am I*

having such a hard time concentrating? Dammit! I'm a risk to the mission, so let me change things up.

"All hands, all hands, training mission change. My suit has undergone a catastrophic failure. You will act as if I cannot move or communicate. This is a training mission change. Kaeden out."

CHAPTER SIX

The sixteen warriors stood in the mech storage area. Their suits had been cleaned, and were recharging.

Terry, Char, and Marcie strolled in together. Kae nodded to his parents and smiled at his wife. She replied by raising one eyebrow.

"Don't tell me this is going to be one of those after-action reviews," Kae grumbled.

Marcie punched him in the chest before playfully pushing him aside. Terry and Char stepped into the spot he vacated.

"Not bad at all," Char started. "I liked how you stayed in formation during your maneuvers. I liked how you placed your explosives, two squads providing security and two doing the job. I don't like how long it took, but practice makes perfect. You'll do more explosives practice on the hangar deck, but you'll do it with gravity in place. Kae, I liked the added pressure of the dead suit. Well done!"

Kae smiled sheepishly. Marcie knew his facial expressions, so she suspected he was holding something back. She didn't have to wait until they were alone to find out.

What was that look you just gave me? she asked via her comm chip.

Nothing. What do you mean? he replied.

Out with it, Kae, Marcie said, wondering if the comm chip properly captured the blend of her wife's and colonel's voices.

I couldn't focus on the mission. I'm worried about Fleeter. I'm worried about this mission. And I'm bone-tired for some reason.

Marcie nodded, squeezed Kae's hand as she leaned against him, and turned her attention back to the debriefing.

"The suits are going to be our future," Terry professed. He inhaled deeply, drawing the air in slowly. He could smell the technology, the metal, the ozone, the cleansers. "The firepower at our command is more than just impressive. It can alter the outcome of any campaign. Look at what we have accomplished—flying through space, engaging an ogre-style tank, fighting a dug-in enemy with advanced weaponry, and more. I don't hesitate to say that with a platoon of these, we can unleash Armageddon on any enemy."

"Unless the enemy has mechs too," Kae said softly, although it sounded loud in the silence.

"And when that time comes, we'll be ready. It's not just the power of these suits. We will always be better because of our training and our minds. All Ten had to do was seal the airlocks and our last mission would have been stillborn. As Timmons and his team discovered, there's nothing that will render you combat-ineffective more quickly than trying to hang on to the outside of a starship speeding through space. Ten simply didn't contemplate the possibility of such an attack."

Marcie would have walked away to take the floor, but Kaeden leaned more heavily against her until she was almost completely supporting his weight. She tried to look casual as she talked.

"When we go to war, we are in it to win. I've been using the Federation's extensive libraries to study battles throughout history. We don't have to kill the enemy soldiers, we just have to eliminate their *will* to fight. The mechs can tie down an army while we conduct surgical small-unit strikes against enemy logistics and their leadership. When we cut Ten's umbilical cord, all those men and the ships' weaponry became useless. After that we mopped up at little risk to our warriors, and now we have added their ships to our fleet."

Marcie stopped, unsure how she wanted to complete her thought, and Kae's eyes rolled back in his head as he slumped.

"What's wrong with him?" Terry asked, jumping forward to help carry his son. Char was instantly there, too.

"Sickbay," Terry declared after a close look at his son.

Marcie didn't hesitate. She heaved Kae over her shoulder and started jogging.

"Gomez, take over," Terry ordered over his shoulder as the group disappeared into the corridor. The fifteen remaining warriors stood in stunned silence.

Enhanced people didn't get sick and pass out.

. . .

Keeg Station

"Do you know why they haven't left yet?" Sue asked. The *War Axe* held its position nearby.

Timmons had gone to *Sheri's Pride* to oversee the installation of Federation hardware to make the ship compatible with Bad Company operations. The gravitic technology on board needed upgrading as well. The new hardware hadn't arrived yet, but Timmons was setting everything up for plug and play when it did, while simultaneously trying to show the men how things worked in their new world.

It had only been two days.

"The mountain of enlightenment is steep and reaches to the heavens." Sue put her hand on the window as if she could touch her mate.

"I think we need to go over there and start beating some sense into those men," Felicity drawled from behind her desk. A cup of coffee sat in front of her. It was the synthesized stuff, but still better than anything they'd had back on Earth until Terry's exploits in the Caribbean had made it possible to bring the occasional bean back to North Chicago. "It's about that time."

Sue nodded. The two women weren't making much progress, but they finally had help.

"Dionysus, if you would be so kind, please connect us with *Sheri's Pride* and stand by to run your first video," Felicity instructed the AI.

"I am at your command. May I say that you look simply magnificent today, Madam Director? Radiant as always," Dionysus replied.

Sue slowly turned and gave Felicity the hairy eyeball.

"What? Ted programmed Dion's stepdaddy, so it's filling in since Ted is gone."

"Ted has never ever in all his existence complimented anyone on how they looked."

Felicity smiled slyly.

"No. Don't you tell me that!" Sue exclaimed with a grin. "My congratulations. I thought he was untrainable."

"It took a while," Felicity drawled, "and he's still a work in progress. I think the kids made the difference."

"How were you two able to have kids? Werewolves usually aren't fertile."

"Maybe it was just meant to be," Felicity replied before her attention was drawn to incessant beeping from her computer. "What?"

"You're broadcasting everything," Timmons said in a hushed voice. "Do you really want to talk about bucking bologna pony rides in front of eleven hundred men who have never known a woman?"

Felicity's cheeks turned bright red and the color drained from Sue's face.

"Good morning," Felicity said with a smile, working to recover her composure. "Today we're going to start with a video which shows how co-workers should interact. We believe that showing you is far better than trying to tell you. Dionysus, please roll the film."

The AI replaced the station director's image with a video of two male workers with toolboxes in a corridor. They worked on a junction box together, talking through the procedure for replacement. When they were done, one thanked the other and they each went their own way. A similar video cued up next, but this time one of the workers was female. Everything in the video was identical except the second worker's sex.

When the clip finished, Felicity's image reappeared onscreen. The men on the ship were seated at the tables watching her, and an inset on her screen showed what they were seeing. Sue finally moved into view, waving over Felicity's shoulder.

"See, gentlemen? That was how an interaction with a female co-worker should go. Treat us the same as you would a male, and you won't have any problems," Sue told them.

Felicity was about to close the link when she saw someone in the crowd with their hand up.

"You there, with your hand raised... Do you have a question?"

"Why do women have long hair?"

Felicity turned to look at Sue, who was self-consciously pulling her long blonde hair back. The director looked back at the screen, resisting the urge to tuck her hair behind her ear. "It's a freedom that we enjoy. There are men with long hair, too," she said weakly.

"Not here. If women want to be treated the same, they should look the same," the man countered.

Felicity started to panic. "That's not how it works. Everyone is different!"

The man waved his arm to take in the mass of bodies on *Sheri's Pride*. "Men." He pointed at the screen. "Women. And if you want us to keep working, we need women!"

Sue's comm device buzzed, and she casually side-stepped until she was out of the camera's eye.

Timmons.

"Yes?" Sue asked quietly.

"Way to go. You've started a riot." Timmons clicked off.

"Guards, please reassert control, but don't hurt any of them. This isn't their fault." Felicity turned off the camera.

"That could have gone better," Sue said. She returned to the window and looked at the speck of light that represented the ship her mate was on. "I hope things don't get out of control."

On board *Sheri's Pride*

The workers were pounding on the tables, a syncopation that threatened to give Timmons a massive headache. He walked to the front of the massive space and held his arms up for silence. One man approached and started yelling in the werewolf's face.

"I suggest you sit the fuck down," Timmons growled.

"Or what?" the emboldened man shouted, leaning close.

Timmons delivered an uppercut to the man's jaw that sent him flying backwards, and he landed unconscious among those seated in the first row. Blood dripped from his mouth; he'd bitten through his tongue from the violence of the blow.

A hush came over the group.

"*LOOK AT YOU!*" Timmons yelled. His face twisted with anger, and he inhaled through clenched teeth before continuing in a calmer voice, "Look at yourselves. You're acting like animals, and that's why there won't be any women over here. There are eleven hundred of you, and women would have no way of protecting themselves if you went for them. Of *course* they are afraid."

The men were paying attention to him. He felt pity for them. "Every culture has gone through this at some time, but I never expected to see it here—the breakdown where men treat women as property. Out here, we're in the future!"

Timmons spread his arms wide.

"And you're acting like Neanderthals. Cut your stupid shit out or I will beat the holy fuck out of each and every one of you!"

Timmons scanned the crowd, making eye contact with as many as would look at him.

"You two, carry him to Sickbay," Timmons told two men in the front row, pointing at the man he'd punched out. The two looked confused.

"I don't know what a sickbay is," one man replied meekly.

"Take him to the shuttle, then. The closest sickbay is on the station, so I guess that's where we'll have to take him. Dammit!" Timmons waved Tim and Brice to him.

"Nice slap-down," Tim said, unperturbed by the near riot.

"Get them to work. I'll escort this knucklehead to the station and be right back." Timmons tapped his pad. "Dionysus, is your handoff from Plato complete? Are you ready to issue the maintenance orders to this mob?"

"I am. Today's schedule starts with routine tasks, and after lunch we'll begin the gravitic engine upgrades," the AI replied.

"What's on the menu?" Timmons asked, suspecting he already knew the answer.

"I won't dignify that with a response," Dionysus confirmed.

"Tasteless protein bars, my favorite! I'll eat when I'm on the station and bring you two something back." Timmons led the way as the two from the front row dragged the unconscious man.

Timmons stopped and looked at the crowd. He rolled his finger at Brice and Tim.

"Stop lollygagging and get to work!" Tim shouted.

Grumbling to themselves, the men pulled out their pads to check on the day's work orders. Under lowered brows, they watched Timmons and the three of their number head out.

Sickbay on the *War Axe*

"Ted, you get your ass up here right-fucking-now!" Terry yelled.

"Language…" the semi-conscious Kaeden mumbled as Marcie rolled him off her shoulder and into the Pod-doc.

The white walls in Sickbay gave it an aura of sterility. It felt high-tech, but not—maybe more of a laboratory.

Char leaned into the Pod-doc and tried to look into Kae's eyes. "Where is Cordelia?" she asked no one in particular, then over her comm chip, *Cory? Can you come to Sickbay, please? And hurry—it's Kaeden.*

I heard. I'm almost there.

Cory raced around the corner and ran into her father, but Terry didn't seem to notice. He looked at his son in disbelief.

"This isn't supposed to happen. The nanos…" He looked

confused. Cory worked past him. She leaned beside her mother and reached into the Pod-doc, putting one hand on Kae's chest. The connection between them started to glow blue like her eyes, which always glowed that color.

"I can't help him," she whispered.

"TED!" Terry roared into the corridor.

"Your bellowing hurts my ears. You sound like a bull in heat," Ted said from nearby.

Ted hurried into Sickbay and went straight to the computer system. "Smedley, plug me in and let's take a look. Everyone, clear away from the Pod-doc."

Marcie yanked off Kae's pants and ducked under the lid as it lowered into place. She looked at the shell of the Kurtherian technology, to which equipment many in the Bad Company owed their lives.

Ted's eyes unfocused as he communed with Smedley, and when the holographic screens came up Ted became embroiled in the advanced technology none of the others understood. Terry stood unmoving and Char joined him, seized his hand in both of hers, and watched the closed Pod-doc. Cory leaned against her father, while Marcie kept one hand on the shell.

Kaeden was inside and something was wrong.

Ted worked without comment as time dragged on.

CHAPTER SEVEN

Keeg Station

"I feel like I'm in Heaven," the man said. His eyes fluttered as he tried to focus on his surroundings. In addition to Timmons, three women stood around him in Keeg Station's sickbay—Felicity, Sue, and a medical technician. Oddly, all three women had long blonde hair.

Sue considered the man. "How do you know about Heaven?"

The man's eyes shot wide in panic. "It's something we talk about where no one else can hear, but we imagine it like this. Angels looking down on us with the glory of the sun. When we get sent to space, we no longer see the sun of Home World."

Felicity's expression softened at his words, and the man reached toward her.

She slapped his hand away. "What do you think you're doing?"

"Your hair is unique. None of the people have hair that

color." He reached toward her again, she slapped his hand away a second time.

"Why do you think you're here?" Felicity asked, shuffling out of arm's reach. Sue followed her out of range.

"Because that guy punched me in the face!" He tried to sound angry, but the Pod-doc had fixed his jaw while he was passed out. He hadn't suffered throughout the ordeal.

"Why do you think he punched you in the face?" Felicity pressed.

The man looked away, shrugging and shaking his head.

"Because of garbage like that. You're trying to touch my hair because I'm different? How about you accept that there are differences and treat me with respect, like you would anyone else you worked with? When you sit around and talk about Heaven, are you touching each other?"

Timmons bit his lip to keep from snickering, and Sue cast a warning glare his way since she was fighting it too.

"I'll be outside," Timmons managed to say, jaw muscles working to stifle a laugh.

"I'll be with him." Sue rushed after her mate, bumping into him when they tried to get through the door at the same time. Timmons patted her butt as she went through and then dodged when she took a swing at his hand.

As the door closed behind them, Felicity rolled her eyes and returned her attention to the man on the gurney.

He contemplated Felicity and the technician, but didn't answer the question.

"I'll tell you why: because you don't get it. What's it going to take for you to understand?"

"Women in our lives," the man replied softly. As he looked at Felicity and the technician tears welled in his eyes, and one escaped and trailed down his cheek. He made no effort to wipe it away.

"My name is Rowan." The technician moved close, letting her hair dangle near his hand. "What's yours?"

He looked at her, confused for a moment, but his features softened as he smiled. "I'm Chris-bo-Runner."

"'Chris Brenner.' Is it okay if I call you Chris?"

"Of course," the man stammered. He nodded toward her hair, and she smiled back. He caressed it gently before rubbing a few strands between his fingers. "So soft."

"It's just like yours."

He started to laugh. "It is not just like mine." He removed his hand and held it up, palm open, as if to show that he didn't take anything. "Women are *not* just like men, but respect for the angels that touch our lives? Yes, we should freely give that. Please accept my apologies. And I even apologize to the mean man who left."

"We're far from angels, sweetie, but that's a start," Felicity drawled.

"If you'd like to show him the station before he has to return to his ship, that would be okay." Felicity waved and started walking away, but stopped and spoke as if talking to the door. "Someone will stay close."

Rowan offered to help Chris off the gurney, so he took her hand and hopped down. She grimaced and cried out, "Not so hard!"

He let go and his mouth fell open. He stood perfectly still, shocked by his transgression. She took his hand.

"Like this."

"I've never held hands with anyone before."

"I figured. Let me show you the wonders of Keeg

Station. Will you have time for lunch before heading back?"

He hesitated. "I don't know, but I don't want to go back to the ship." He hung his head. "I don't want this moment to end."

"All moments end, Chris," Rowan whispered. "What matters is what we do with the ones we have, and then what we do when we have more."

The *War Axe*

The holo screens dropped. Ted rubbed his hands and started to leave, but Terry blocked his path.

"You big bully!" Ted exclaimed.

Char forced her way between the two. "You were going to leave without telling us what is going on? As your alpha, I demand that you tell us."

"Fine," Ted said, raising his head to glare at the taller Terry Henry. "His nanocytes were infected with some kind of degenerative code. In biological terms, he had the flu. Once the malicious code was removed, his nanos went back to work, but they are taking an excess of energy from his body to repair the damage that they did while in their degenerative state. Repairing that is taking all his energy and making him weak right now."

"So he's going to be fine?" Marcie asked, relieved.

"Yes." Ted tried to push Terry aside, but the colonel wouldn't budge.

"You'll leave when I say you can leave," Char said

Ted leaned back and crossed his arms. "All these years, and I may have been wrong. I always assumed he was the bully first, but it appears that you may have been out-bullying him all along, Charumati."

Char's eyes were starting to glow purple, which was an indicator of her anger.

"Ted, if we've ever bullied you, we apologize. That being said, I as the alpha give direction to the pack. Period. If you were the alpha you'd give direction, and we'd listen and obey. It is our way. Maybe you think you've been bullied because we have gone farther and farther from the usual arrangement. I concede that you have your own life now and wish you the best with it, but there are still times —like now—where pack business takes precedent. If you would be so kind as to answer my questions, I would appreciate it. Will anyone else catch this nano disease?"

Char spoke calmly, but clenched and unclenched her fists. She didn't see how Kaeden had become afflicted in the first place, and she was afraid that the others would be susceptible.

Ted uncrossed his arms. "I don't know the answer to that. I thought you wanted me to deal with what was bothering Kaeden."

"Yes, of course, but now that he's supposedly cured..." Char looked at the still-closed Pod-doc before continuing, "we need to make sure we're not responding to another emergency like this later today or tomorrow for many of us at once. Imagine if this happened while we were on Benitus Seven, everyone with nanos going down? Do you know how many that is?"

Ted nodded unemotionally. He knew exactly how many that was.

"All of us," Marcie whispered before finding her voice.

"All of us! Please, Uncle Ted, fix this so it doesn't happen again," she pleaded.

Ted shook his head. He didn't want to take the time, but knew that he had to because he was Ted—the only one who could solve the problem. They needed him. Ted lifted his chin high and gruffly replied, "Okay."

He returned to his position, opened a holographic matrix, and got to work.

"Have you notified Nathan?" Char asked.

"Yes. He said his AI was linked with Smedley to get the raw data. I'll update him with Kae's condition when we know more."

"With good news. We'll update him with good news," Char clarified.

The Pod-doc opened and Marcie hurried in. Kae's eyes were clear, but he sat up slowly.

"What happened?" he asked.

"Your nanos got sick. You'll need some rack time to recover," Marcie told him as she held his head in her hands and peered deeply into his eyes. He winked at her and looked over her shoulder at his parents.

"Hey, Mom!" he said weakly. "I'm naked."

Char and Terry both smiled and turned away so he could get dressed. The werewolves had never worried about anyone seeing them naked. It was a part of who they were, since the clothes didn't transition with them to their Were forms. Kaeden had never fully embraced nakedness, even though he'd seen the pack, including his mother, without their clothes more times than he could count.

With Marcie's help, Kae dressed and then left what passed for the ship's sickbay. Ted continued working.

"We can't start the mission until we know this thing isn't going to bite us," Terry said. "I want to see his suit. Maybe there's something in it that can give us a hint where this thing came from. And where the hell is Ankh?"

"He is working on the interstellar communication problem. Ted said he couldn't let it languish at this critical juncture," Smedley informed them.

Char nodded darkly and followed Terry out.

Fitzroy circled Bundin. The Podder waved his tentacles, but didn't need to rotate to keep the human where he could see him.

The sergeant jumped forward, hopped off Bundin's shell, and drove a solid front kick into his stalk. Two of the Podder's tentacles whipped out and grabbed Fitzroy's leg. They twisted and then spun, whipping Fitzroy in a spiral that ended when he landed in a pile on the floor.

Bundin leaned forward to protect his soft underbelly before Fitzroy got back into the match.

But Fitzroy wasn't getting up. Joseph and Petricia stepped onto the mat and pulled the sergeant to his feet.

"Hand-to-hand combat with aliens isn't ever going to be straightforward," Joseph said, looking at the warriors' faces around the ring. "You have to find their vulnerabilities during the fight, and can have no preconceived notions. Did you see at the end how Bundin bent over when Fitzroy was on the ground?"

Some heads nodded, but others hadn't noticed Bundin's subtle move.

"Tell them why you did that."

"To protect my soft undershell. Had Fitzroy been able to get beneath me, I would not have been able to see him or protect my ears and brain from an attack. We have a very soft spot under there where our auditory sensor is located."

"And there you have it. Creatures instinctively protect their vulnerabilities, so you should look for it and exploit it."

"All while getting the snot kicked out of you," Fitzroy added.

"Yes, if you're taking on an enemy one to one. I recommend you hunt in teams."

"Hunt?" someone said from the audience.

"Yes. You all know my proclivity for using precise language. It's a gift and a curse. In this case, I believe you'll be hunting the interdimensional interlopers, since they are not armed like us. Our mechs could very well wreak havoc, and if so I would expect them to run. In that case they'll have to be hunted, but what is the most dangerous thing you can face?"

"A cornered and wounded enemy," Fitzroy answered.

Kimber stepped onto the mat.

"These creatures look like bipeds, and they have two arms. They could fight just like us, or completely different. They have horns on their heads, so their skulls may be inordinately thick and well-protected. One advantage is our comm chips." Kim tapped her head. "Whoever is first to fight one of these, share how you defeated it. There is no sense in each of us learning the same lesson. Smedley?"

"Yes, Major Kimber? I standby to serve."

"How about if you consolidate the input from the platoon as they engage the enemy—assuming we'll be conducting a search and destroy mission as the colonel believes."

"I will consolidate and disseminate, demonstrate my ability to concentrate, never equate that which we can dominate!" Smedley rapped.

Kimber looked at Joseph and Petricia, who shook their heads. Aaron and Yanmei shrugged, and Christina pursed her lips and whistled, then said, "Smedley? Are you okay, buddy? All kinds of weird shit is coming out of your virtual mouth."

"I'm sorry, but Major Kaeden has been listening to some interesting Earth music from before the fall. I don't think I have the hang of it," Smedley replied.

"No, and don't do that again. It makes me think you're going to have a seizure." Christina twisted her mouth as if she was eating a lemon.

"I'm not sure I can have a seizure," General Smedley Butler replied.

"I didn't think my brother could get sick, either, but that happened," Kim interjected.

"Yes, and Ted has been magnificent as usual in tracking down and eliminating the virus. I will be scheduling everyone for time in the Pod-doc to upgrade their nanocytes when Ted gives me the go-ahead. It will be an inoculation."

"We're getting a shot, people!" Kim called. Most had no

idea what she was talking about. She only knew because of the stories that her adoptive parents Terry and Char used to tell.

"A shot at what, the red devils? Just tell me where to aim!" a bold warrior said.

"It may be as simple as that, or it may be orders of magnitude more complex," Smedley replied.

"Never mind. I'll pick my own targets, and those bastards can stand-the-fuck-by. Say hello to my little friend! And the last word we'll hear from them will be 'Incoming.'" The man crossed his arms and looked smug.

Kim slapped him on the arm as she walked past on her way to size up the platoon.

"What did you hard-chargers learn today?" she shouted.

"If you watch your enemy closely, he'll show you where his vulnerabilities are."

Kim looked at Joseph, who smiled and nodded. She gave him the thumbs up.

"What else?" she asked, turning slowly to see if anyone wanted to answer. She kept her hand on Bundin's shell. The blue stalk-headed alien was becoming a friend to them all.

"I suggest that we have gained a taste for winning," the Podder offered.

"What do you mean by that?" Kim asked, looking into the closest of Bundin's four eyes.

"An army that is worried about losing takes more care in the fight, doing what must be done to improve its chances. An army that expects to win may fail to take necessary risks." Bundin waved two of his four tentacle-arms to add emphasis to his statement. The other two crossed, with hands folded in front.

"Most profound, Master Podder," Joseph said.

"Are we resting on our laurels?" Kimber demanded, hammering a fist into her hand. "Are we taking the enemy for granted? I hope not, or you'll feel the sting of my wrath!"

The room was silent. "Have you been watching too much television lately?" Joseph asked as he stepped forward, held Kimber by her shoulders, and stared deep into her eyes. "They say that stuff will pollute your mind!"

Kimber shrugged Joseph off. "Pollute my mind? Living with Auburn has polluted my sinuses, but that's something completely different."

"I heard that!" Auburn yelled from the back of the room. He knew what she meant. Their first ten years together had been spent raising cattle, and the smell of the stockyards had been overwhelming at times.

Christina snickered.

"I never questioned my choices," she called back.

"No more TV for you!" he countered.

"Good session, Joseph," Kimber said quickly before they lost the attention span of the group for good. "Aaron and Yanmei, anything to add?"

Aaron nodded and stepped forward. "Lao Tzu taught that to become learned, each day one should add something. To become enlightened, each day one should drop something. He means you should rid yourself of the baggage that is weighing you down; the extra notions that are holding you back. If you approach this coming battle with an open mind you'll flex more quickly. As Terry Henry Walton has taught us, the one who can decide what to do quickest is the one who wins the fight." The weretiger bowed deeply to the platoon and returned to his place behind the ranks.

Kimber contemplated what he had said, unsure if any of the platoon understood even though he had explained.

"Bad Company, exporting justice. Platoon, *dismissed.*" Kimber patted Bundin's shell as she watched the platoon break into smaller groups. Many continued their workout with free weights and weight machines, and others started stretching in preparation for running laps on the hangar deck. To make it interesting, they always increased the deck's gravity to one hundred and fifty percent of normal.

Fitzroy and one other worked their way to Aaron and Yanmei.

"How does one clear clutter from the mind? Teach me, *sensei.*" Fitzroy had his hands together as if praying.

The weretigers looked at each other. The Chinese didn't say '*sensei,*' but they knew what he meant. The edges of Yanmei's mouth twitched upward and she nodded once.

"We shall, padawan," Aaron replied, choosing the word for student from the Star Wars lexicon.

Everything was relative.

"Meet us at nine tonight for your first lesson in meditation," Yanmei instructed.

Fitzroy almost argued, since showtime for morning calisthenics was at four, but caught himself and bowed slightly instead. "See you then."

Fitzroy and the second man strolled away, moving from warrior to warrior and providing encouragement as a platoon sergeant was supposed to do.

Kimber joined the weretigers. "You have a disciple?"

"It appears we do," Aaron agreed. He wrapped an arm around Yanmei's shoulders. "And now if you'll excuse us, we need to figure out exactly what we're going to do with him."

The couple bowed their heads politely, and holding hands, they headed from the recreation room which the warriors also called their workout room.

Joseph and Petricia were deep into a conversation with Bundin about his observations of human behavior and motivation. Fear and confidence—how could the two go hand in hand?

Christina joined Kimber. "I'll excuse myself too. I have been watching this one show, and can't get enough of it. I need to see what happens before we get to Benitus. Ta ta!"

Kimber watched her leave and listened to the warriors talk among themselves for a while, but couldn't focus. She was still worried about her brother.

Which reminded her. "Has anyone seen Shonna and Merrit?"

Shrugs and head-shakes.

Smedley, I need you to check on Shonna and Merrit right now, please.

They are in their quarters and appear to be sleeping.

Wake them up and tell them I'm on my way. Kimber raced from the recreation room, leaving wondering glances in her wake.

After a few moments, Smedley replied, *I cannot wake them up.*

Notify my parents and raise the alarm.

The emergency klaxons sounded before she took

another step, and she accelerated as only the enhanced could up one flight of stairs and down a long corridor. When she turned into the alcove where their room was located, she found Terry and Char already there.

Dokken was sniffing the door.

"*Smedley, override the damn door!*" Terry yelled.

The door slid open and they hurried in. Shonna and Merrit were in bed, alive but in comas. Terry lifted Merrit from the bed and tossed him over his shoulder and Char took Shonna. Kimber led the way as the two loped down the hallway, trying to limit the impact on the unconscious Weres.

When they reached what they were calling "Sickbay," Ted was still embroiled within his holographic field. TH stepped aside to let Char put Shonna into the Pod-doc first. After quickly stripping off Shonna's clothes, Char stepped back and closed the lid.

"*TED!*" she yelled.

The holo images shimmered and then dropped.

"What? I'm doing what you ordered: looking for a way to inoculate the rest against this thing."

"Shonna is in a coma in the Pod-doc and needs you, and Merrit is right behind her." Char pointed. Ted looked surprised.

Without a word, he raised the screens again and got to work.

"Does that mean he's fixing Shonna?" Kim asked.

Terry shrugged as much as he could with Merrit over one shoulder. He carefully laid the werewolf on the deck and stood protectively over him.

Char put her ear to the Pod-doc. "I think it's working." She continued to listen to the machine.

They stood where they were, since no one wanted to move and break Ted's concentration.

When the captain showed up, the three shushed him. Terry pointed to his own head so they could bring him up to speed using the comm chip.

CHAPTER EIGHT

Keeg Station

"A virus is affecting the nanocytes of the older generation," Dionysus explained patiently.

Felicity held her hand over her open mouth. Older generation—people like her and Ted.

"Ted is working on a solution right now. With some effort he can fix the nanocytes within the individuals, but that is a tailored solution and may only provide temporary relief. He is working on a long-term fix, but he can't make progress on that while working on the individuals. However, the more individuals who succumb to the virus, the more data Ted will have from which to extrapolate a more robust remedy."

"Did Ted program you? You sound just like him," Felicity drawled. Her lips trembled as she added, "I miss him already."

"As an AI, Madam Director, I am evolved. I received some consistent base programming from my father Plato. The resemblance to anything else is merely a coincidence, probably because we share the same love of logic," Dionysus explained.

"No need to go on, I get it. You are members of the brotherhood—kindred spirits—but none of that matters right now. Are we going to get sick and die?" Felicity sat with her hands folded in her lap. Her motivation for doing anything had been crushed.

"I see that you are worried, Madam Director, and I can assure you that one hundred percent of the time, worrying does not solve the problem."

Felicity looked at her computer screen, where Dionysus was showing a video of puppies playing in fresh-cut grass. "You said you were evolved, but then you told me that worry doesn't solve problems. You really sound like my husband, and there are times when I don't consider him evolved at all."

"Ted is the highest form of life we've ever encountered."

"All hail Ted!" Felicity drawled sarcastically.

"All hail Ted!" Dionysus repeated.

"Stop that, you stupid electronic bucket of bolts. I asked if we are going to get sick and die and you never answered so now I demand an answer." Felicity tried to push her monitor away, but stopped when the video changed to a kitten pushing a cup off a counter. She chuckled. It had been a long time since she'd had a cat.

"I can hear from the emotion in your tone that you don't want a probability calculation. You want to hear the word 'no,' and that is what I will tell you. No, Madam Director, you will not get sick and die, because Ted and Plato will fix the problem. I will embrace that calculation because they have never failed."

Felicity rubbed her chin, then stood and went to the window. She took a deep breath, feeling the strength of her enhanced being. She couldn't remember what it was like to be sick.

She knew she should be terrified, but Ted was working on it. That thought gave her the comfort she sought.

The *War Axe*

Terry sat on the deck in the corridor outside Sickbay. It had been seven hours, and neither Ted nor Shonna nor Merrit had emerged. Char was sleeping with her head in his lap, and Dokken was curled against them both.

Terry thought back to the early days when he had slept between Clyde the dog and Charumati the werewolf. They both put off so much heat that he had often taken to the floor as a refuge. Since they had lived in the Wasteland, the heat was a constant presence. Over time, it became a comfortable blanket in which he wrapped himself.

TH stroked Char's hair and scratched Dokken's fuzzy ears, but neither roused so he leaned his head back and dozed off.

"Bring the shuttle in," Micky instructed.

Clifton issued the instructions while Smedley opened the hangar doors.

"I'm going down to meet them." Micky climbed from his chair and walked off the bridge, but as soon as the hatch closed behind him he started to run. Terry had reminded him of what he had learned as a junior officer in the Empire's service.

When the boss runs, everyone panics.

Micky was panicking. He wasn't sure what the affliction was, but the Bad Company was in complete lockdown. Training had been dialed back.

Way back.

The warriors were spending time in individual pursuits because they had no idea how the virus was being transmitted. Only three had been ill, but two more were inbound. Felicity was escorting Sue and Timmons to the *War Axe*, where Ted continued to work on curing that which plagued the werewolves. Kae was an outlier, as the only non-Were to fall ill.

Not knowing was what was causing it made them all afraid.

Micky vaulted down the stairs, taking them three at a time. He slowed as he passed the deck with the Pod-doc. Terry and Char were down there.

Waiting.

The captain continued to descend. When he reached the hangar level, he slowed to a brisk walk before going through the hatch. It wouldn't do to look flushed and out of breath. Even though there was a medical emergency, there was nothing that could be done with the new patients until Ted was ready.

Micky took a deep breath and entered the hangar. The shuttle had maneuvered until it was right outside the hatch, and he almost walked into a pair of workers from Keeg Station who were carrying one stretcher. Sue's blonde hair trailed over the edge of that one, and Timmons was unconscious on a second stretcher. Felicity walked behind them, but she didn't look as distraught as Micky would have expected.

When the station director saw Micky, she nodded and approached him.

"Time to light this candle," Felicity drawled softly. "I believe my husband is working on the cure, so let's go see him." She didn't wait for Micky as she waved for the others to follow.

She'd been on board the *War Axe* during the transit from Earth, so she knew her way around. Micky followed the group as they climbed.

They departed the stairs on the correct deck and continued their parade toward the ship's small sickbay.

Terry lifted his eyes slowly as the group approached. Felicity stopped and took a knee next to him.

"You've looked better," she told him before leaning in for a half-hug.

Dokken raised his head, but his second eyelid was half closed and his tongue hung sideways out of his mouth. Char sat up and yawned.

"Any news?" Char asked.

"Not as far as I know," Terry replied. He looked hopefully to Felicity, but she shook her head.

"He's in there." It wasn't a question. Felicity held up a finger to those carrying the stretchers to indicate they should wait.

She went through the hatch, stopping while still outside Ted's holographic screens. Shonna lay on the floor, and Merrit was nowhere to be seen.

After a short scuffle in the corridor during which

Dokken expressed his displeasure at being moved, Terry and Char stepped into the room.

When they saw Shonna, they picked her up. She was groggy, but at their touch she opened her eyes.

"Better?" Terry asked.

"On the mend," she mumbled.

Felicity looked through the holos at Ted, who seemed to dance as he touched points within his three-dimensional space. He didn't look good, and he winced as he moved. He squinted from red eyes set within a tortured visage.

Felicity slapped a hand over her mouth and looked at him in horror. She started to reach through the matrix, but Char jumped up and grabbed her arm. The two stood frozen in the moment as they watched Ted and his superhuman efforts.

Terry stood with Shonna in his arms.

The holo screens fell, and the Pod-doc started to open.

Felicity leapt forward, catching Ted before he collapsed. His eyes sparkled briefly, and he weakly reached up and touched her hair.

She shook her head and smiled as she started to cry.

"Pod-doc," he whispered before he passed out.

She didn't hesitate. She lifted Ted and shuffled around the computer equipment. After Char pulled Merrit from the bed Felicity put her husband inside, and manually closed the cover.

The system started automatically.

"Plato, are you here?" Terry asked.

"I am, Colonel Walton. We have developed what we believe is an automated process to scrub the bad code from the nanocytes. That code has become deeply embedded and is quite virulent, fighting off the upgraded code as if that were the virus. It's hard to believe this isn't a malicious attempt to remove the enhancements the nanocytes bring to the human body."

"Does everyone have the bad code, and how did we get it?"

"We believe it was introduced at Keeg Station, where it was ingested and then started to spread. I believe everyone will get it except Charumati and Cordelia, since their nanocytes are unique.

"There may be a biological solution if the infestation is caught quickly enough, but the real fix is in the reprogramming to ensure none of the malicious code remains."

"Is that what you're doing now with Ted?" Felicity asked.

"Yes, and the process has been streamlined. Ted's nanocytes should be repaired within a few minutes, then we can cycle everyone else through. Ted has optimized the process based on information gathered from the first few victims. Ted is a genius," Plato added.

"All hail Ted," Felicity muttered.

"All hail Ted!" Plato replied.

"I don't even want to know," Char said, shaking her head before smiling at her husband. "Crisis averted?"

"Almost," TH replied. "Smedley, get every swinging dick up here for a turn in the Pod-doc, starting with the tactical teams and ending with the platoon."

"Only the man members, sir?" the general asked.

"What? No. All the members. What makes you ask that?"

95

"Did I take the term 'swinging dicks' too literally? You said that you want all the members?"

Shonna and Merrit each grinned as widely as they could and gave Terry thumbs-ups.

"I think he is messing with you," Char said as the first group arrived with Kim in the lead. "Queue them up and send them through as fast as they can be processed."

The Pod-doc lid popped, and Felicity forced her way inside. She picked Ted up and maneuvered through the room, trying not to bang Ted's head against the wall on her way out.

Kimber looked at the men with the two stretchers. "We'll take care of them from here. Go to the mess deck and get yourselves something to eat. I think Jenelope is cooking a special meal as a morale booster."

The four men glanced both ways down the corridor, but didn't move.

Kim pointed and gave them directions and the captain, who had been standing to the side, stepped up. "I'll show them the way. I could use a little something myself."

Micky San Marino walked past, feeling much better than when he had first arrived at the sickbay.

Aaron and Yanmei brought Sue in first, and Kim moved the curtain that had been shoved aside to give the unconscious werewolf some privacy. The weretigers put Sue into the Pod-doc and removed the stretcher while Plato worked his technological magic on her. When she was finished, Kimber helped her out while Aaron and Yanmei carried Timmons in. When he had been reprogrammed, Aaron looked at Yanmei and pointed to the open Pod-doc.

"You first," Aaron said.

Yanmei tried to get Aaron to go next, but he refused.

"Let it go," Joseph said softly to the weretigers.

Petricia followed suit by urging Joseph to go before her.

"Let it go." Petricia repeated his words.

"I'm not sure I like this game," Joseph admitted before caving in. "Thank you, my love. I will go first so that I can lift you in should you become ill."

Joseph bowed slightly, and Petricia tipped her head in reply.

"Will you lift *me* in?" Yanmei asked.

"Fine, I'll go first," Aaron said, giving Joseph the hairy eyeball.

"Out of my way! Werewolf coming through. If y'all are going to dilly-dally, I'm gonna get this knocked out. My television isn't going to watch itself," Christina declared.

"Why are you talking like that?" Terry asked.

Christina waved him away as she stripped on the run and swan-dived into the Pod-doc. The lid closed.

"I'll go next." Aaron shrugged out of his clothes and stood behind the curtain.

Terry and Char studied the group in the corridor, family and friends all. Ramses and Auburn were in line behind the others, and Cory was by her husband's side.

"I guess you're immune," TH told his daughter.

"That's what I hear. Good genes or something like that." She nodded, but didn't move. Her knuckles were white from squeezing Ramses' hand.

"It'll be all right. Ted has defeated this thing. We'll rest up and be on our way—go save the universe, and all that." Terry cupped Cory's face in one hand as Merrit draped an arm over the colonel's other shoulder.

"It's what we do," Cory replied softly. "Because there isn't anyone else to do it in this whole universe, is there, Dad?"

Terry looked both ways to confirm that only his inner circle was there. "I've talked with General Reynolds, and there are a number of teams out here, doing what we're doing—exporting justice—but they are only the size of our tac teams. The general wouldn't tell me where they are, but know that we're not alone."

Cory smiled and threw her head back, sending her hair behind her wolf ears. "That's nice to know."

"Shhh. Don't tell anyone." Terry smiled as he followed Char down the corridor on their way to deposit Shonna and Merrit in their room.

Cory watched her parents carrying their friends.

"What the hell was up with that 'All hail Ted' bullshit?" Cory heard her father ask.

"Language!" Ramses shouted over his shoulder. "Dammit, TH, you're killing me. Next time I'll bet against you, because you suck at not swearing!"

CHAPTER NINE

Felicity didn't want to let go, even though Ted kept trying to pull away.

"Are you in a hurry to get away from me?" Felicity asked ominously.

Ted relaxed. "I have work to do. I've lost two days because of the attack on the nanocytes. I want you to be able to talk with your children," Ted argued.

"*We* want to talk with *our* children," Felicity clarified.

Ted waved dismissively at his wife.

She pulled his face to hers and kissed him much longer than he was comfortable with.

Marcie started to laugh, since Ted looked like a child trying to escape his grandmother's embrace. She slapped Ted on the back, and he bumped his forehead against Felicity's. They each held a hand to their heads.

"I'm sorry I couldn't make it down earlier, Mother. Kae was pretty weak," Marcie said.

Kaeden stood behind his wife, looking refreshed after an extra day recovering. Once he'd eaten his fill his recovery had been miraculous, as were that of the others. They had decided to get together and wish Felicity well as she returned to Keeg Station.

"Don't you take him into any of your battles, Terry Henry Walton!" Felicity shook her finger at the colonel. "And no swearing! You're a bad influence on the kids."

"But they're old," Terry countered, earning him a withering look from Kimber and Marcie. "Son of a glitch. Icehole. Mortar forker. I've never sworn in my life! Everyone simply mishears me!"

Felicity put her hands on her hips and gave TH her best disbelieving mother's look. Freed from her grasp, Ted bolted. His wife watched him go.

"Now look what you made me do!"

Marcie took the opportunity to give her mother a hug. Sue and Timmons slapped hands as they passed the group.

"Everyone's getting all shmoopy on us. Fuck off!" Timmons called with a big smile.

"That's what you get for saving his life," Sue said.

"Timmons at his finest," Char replied.

The small group stood in the hangar bay outside a standard Federation shuttle. The two stretchers had been broken down and were stored beneath the seats, so there was a good amount of empty space. Four men waved from the inside as Sue and Timmons took their seats.

They were ready to return to their home. Felicity was too, but she wanted to take her family and friends with her.

"Don't make me kick you out of Seymour Heine's again." She shook a warning finger at him.

Terry ignored her jibe. "Plato has transferred the information to Dionysus, so you can inoculate everyone on board the station."

Felicity frowned, but nodded. "That was some nasty business. I hope it dies here."

"Me, too. I can't imagine what would happen if that were unleashed upon someone like Nathan or General Reynolds."

Felicity waved good-bye and entered the shuttle, then the ramp closed and the hangar bay doors opened. The shuttle lifted off the deck using its gravitic thrusters and accelerated smoothly through the energy field into space.

"About that time?" Char asked.

"Yeah. We have a war to fight. We're on our way to hell to take on the demons."

"It seems like we were just here, but that was a long time ago," Kae suggested as he studied the woodgrain of the captain's conference table.

"Almost a whole lifetime ago." Marcie stood behind her husband and leaned over him just enough so he could rest his head against her. Shonna and Merrit also had seats at the table. They didn't need them, they said, but Terry wouldn't have it any other way.

He stood behind Char after she sat.

"It's time to take the fight to the enemy. They are coming through the tear, and we need to stop that. We have to get back on track and focus on the mission. Kaeden, are you ready to conduct the ground-level reconnaissance?"

"Ready to recce, Colonel," Kae replied.

Marcie looked uncomfortable. "I can take it if Kae's not ready," she suggested, but there was no force behind her words.

Terry looked from one to the other. "I would like to put you in the sky to extract Kae's team if things go south while doing a little recon of your own, but okay. Kimber gets the airborne gig and you'll join Kae's team. Also, Shonna and Merrit, suit up. You'll round out the four mechs. We need a solid group of people who can see creatures who draw power from the Etheric. Kae will lead the team, and you three will spy out what he cannot.

"Joseph, you and Petricia will be in the drop ship with Kimber, just in case there's an opportunity to get inside one of the creatures' heads. The rest of us will be in the combat information center—the CIC space—with a three-dimensional map so we can start planning the attack. We need numbers and locations of the creatures, and the location of the tear. No preconceived notions—I don't know if it looks like a slit, a doorway, or a black freaking hole, but I expect it'll have a distinct energy signature. Hell, we may be able to see it from space."

"I've never worked for you before, Kae, but I have been under you a few times," Marcie whispered. Everyone heard, because there wasn't a single person in the room who wasn't enhanced in one way or another.

Char snickered and looked away.

"He's the mech team leader, so he's in charge. It's how we task organize. I don't see the issue." Terry was confused.

"Dad!" Kae fought valiantly to avoid making eye contact with anyone, and Marcie smiled behind him.

Terry looked to Char for support, so she made a circle with her forefinger and thumb and stabbed into it with the pointer finger of her other hand. After the third time, Terry grabbed her hand.

"Moving right along." The chuckling in the room died down, but Kaeden's face remained red. Terry moved his head until he could see Christina with both eyes. "I want you with me. The challenge we'll face is to plan a major attack with a bunch of minor skirmishes. I'm curious if Pricolici Christina might be the best way we can engage these things in the wild, and I want you to think how we can manage that."

"You want me to hunt them all down by myself? I'm your huckleberry!"

Kae nodded knowingly. "My favorite movie." He held his thumb over his head so Christina could see it from her spot against the wall.

"I am sorry, Colonel Walton," Bundin interjected. "I doubt I'll be much help running around a forest. I believe that I might be better off guarding any prisoners while keeping our drop ship safe. I can fire four blasters simultaneously with a great deal of accuracy."

"Excellent points, Bundin. Your commitment to rear-area security is greatly appreciated, and we bow to your four-eyed abilities."

Terry smiled at the Podder as he started to pace again.

"Bundin shows what I was so ham-handedly trying to put together—everyone to their strengths. If a dog were judged on its ability to climb a tree, it would forever be considered a moron."

Dokken yipped.

"Exactly." Terry wasn't sure if Dokken was agreeing or disagreeing. "Skipper, can the *War Axe* pinpoint a target on the planet's surface using the main weapons?"

Micky rolled his head as he thought about the answer. "If you're thinking about using the ship as close air support, you can forget it. I don't think I can express how far away from the target you would need to be to guarantee your safety. Angle of incidence equals the angle of reflection, right?"

Terry nodded. "Of course, like a light shining off a mirror, but we're talking about refraction here—how the atmosphere could deflect the inbound plasma."

"The atmosphere is in a constant state of flux. We can improve our chances if we are in a geosynchronous orbit directly over the target, but I would still encourage you to be as far away as possible, as in not even on the planet if we fire the mains at a dimensional tear."

"I can buy that, but what does reflection have to do with it?"

"Nothing at all. I was just checking to see if you were paying attention."

"Is that you, Smedley? Have you hijacked the captain?"

Keeg Station

When the gate formed on the side of the *War Axe* away from the station the ship accelerated across the event horizon, shimmered for a moment, and was gone.

"I guess that's that," Sue said.

Felicity strolled over to stand beside the blonde werewolf.

"Do you know what the last words Ted said to me before we came back to the station were?" Felicity asked.

Sue thought for a moment, then shrugged.

"Not a damn thing. He couldn't wait to get back to his lab!"

Sue pulled Felicity to her until they bumped shoulders. "That's the Ted I know."

"Here we are, a wife and her husband's ex, watching my man go away."

"You've worked wonders with him. He's almost good boyfriend material now, but I'm taken." Sue snorted and looked down. "Timmons is almost good boyfriend material, too. They both have their moments, don't they?"

"That they do, my friend. I think it's time to make a personal appearance on *Sheri's Pride*."

"I don't want to, but I know it's the right thing to do. Maybe we can take that medical technician. What's her name?"

"Rowan. And Chris was the nice man that Timmons beat up."

"Isn't that pleasant? They seemed to be getting along well. Too bad they ate at that Seppukarian place. I did not envy the bots cleaning up the projectile vomit," Felicity drawled.

"Chalk that up under 'Worst first dates ever.' I wonder if she did that on purpose?"

"We'll never know. Tell Timmons to saddle up our ride. We've got places to go and people to see."

Benitus Gravity Well

"Ship systems normal. No contacts," K'Thrall reported remotely from the CIC. Micky sat in the captain's chair on the raised dais on the bridge, looking at the empty systems officer position.

He remained torn about manning the CIC, since he was old school. *A captain's place was on the bridge.*

"Clear. You can remove your hoods now," Micky directed. He slipped his over his head and let it retract the rest of the way into the pouch at the back of his collar. "Smedley, bring up a tactical display."

A three-dimensional representation of the system appeared at the front of the bridge. Eleven planets orbited a G-class star, which was bigger and burned hotter than the Earth's sun. This extended the hot zone where five inhospitable planets orbited. Two circled within the habitable zone, and four more planets orbited farther out. Eleven planets, but the only one that mattered was Benitus Seven.

"No other ships within the system? Nothing strange going on?" Micky moved from his chair to the middle of the bridge. He stood behind Clifton as they looked at the innocuous planets orbiting a relatively nondescript star.

"There is a space station in orbit around the seventh planet, but it is not generating signals in a way that we can detect."

"Nice clarification, Smedley. Is that your way of saying that if they are using the Etheric we're not detecting it?"

"Our sensors can detect shifts in Etheric energy, but we aren't seeing anything from the station. The lights are on, but it looks like nobody's home."

"No ships or satellites in orbit?"

"There are satellites, but they seem to be in a similar state as the space station. I detect no ships, but we'll have to get much closer before I can confirm my initial findings. At that time, I'll also be able to scan the planet's surface for other facilities."

"Ask Terry Henry if he'd join me on the bridge, please," Micky requested.

"He'll be here momentarily," the general replied.

On cue, the colonel walked through the hatch with his full entourage.

"What do you think we're looking at, Micky?" Terry asked as he walked over to the captain to study the map.

"A space station and satellites. I'm not amused by the intel we're getting, TH."

Terry ground his teeth before forcing himself to stop, and twisted his mouth to ease the tension in his jaw. "Smedley, can you call Nathan for me, please?"

The connection rang through and Nathan replied in a sleepy voice in audio-only mode. "Hello, what?"

"Nathan, Terry Henry Walton here. We've arrived in the Benitus System. Did you know there was a space station orbiting the planet?"

"Who is this?"

"It's Terry! Wake up, Nathan! How advanced are these people?"

"Terry? Oh, Terry. Yes. How are you doing?"

"Holy butt crumbs, Nathan! Did you set us up again? Don't make me pull the plug on this mission."

"Cool your jets, TH," Nathan said slowly. "What's got you so spun up?"

"A space station and satellites in orbit around Benitus Seven."

"A space station, you say? I didn't know that. We haven't been there before. The *War Axe* is the first Federation ship to visit."

"We're going to take it slow, Nathan. I'm not rushing into this. That space station looks alive, but dead. How far have these creatures infiltrated into Beniton society?"

"Those are all questions that you are in a far better position to answer than me. Is there a reason you woke me out of a sound sleep besides the fact that you wanted to vent your spleen?" Nathan said in a cold and hard voice.

"Fuck, Nathan!" Terry lamented.

"Language!" someone said behind Terry.

"Do we have remote drones that we can send into a system to collect data before we show up alone and unafraid?"

"This isn't Star Wars, Terry. We use real science here. Without the Etheric power source and miniaturized gate technology we can't put a drone into such remote space, so no, we can't send a remote drone unless you can make a deal with the Benitons and get that power source! Then, and only then, we'll see if *R2D2* can build us an unmanned scout ship to be your no-risk advance party."

"You have a way of throwing ice water on a perfectly good tirade," Terry mumbled.

"Is Ramses there?" Nathan asked. Terry held up his hands in confusion. He didn't know if Nathan could see him.

"Right here, Mister Lowell," Ramses called.

Cory started to laugh.

"How am I doing?"

Ramses had his pad in his hand and made an annotation before scrolling. "You're up two hundred and eighty-four credits."

"I knew you couldn't stop yourself, TH. I shake my head in dismay at the misplaced faith your family has in your willpower. You will drag your dying carcass through broken glass to fight an enemy, but you are incapable of stopping yourself from swearing. I suspect there are different parts of the brain involved. I'm going to have to contemplate what to do with all those credits. Cha-ching! Cha-ching! They keep ringing up."

Terry glared at the blank screen before turning around to face Ramses. "Butthole."

Ramses and Cory turned to each other, and in unison they shook their heads and sighed.

"We'll leave you to it, Nathan. You have an empire to oversee, and I'm sure you have more schoolchildren to bilk out of their lunch money."

"Only if they buy our Coke products. Nathan out."

Micky tried not to look at the colonel.

"What are you knuckleheads looking at?" Terry scowled. "I have no dignity left. People are getting their digs in from across the universe! How many are in this betting pool?"

"Almost a thousand at last count," Ramses said softly.

Someone snickered.

"I see how it is. Time to take things seriously. I'm here to chew bubblegum and kick some serious buttocks, and I'm fresh out of bubblegum!" Terry declared before turning back to the graphical representation of the star system.

"When will we be close enough to get a better sensor picture?" TH asked.

"A few hours," Micky replied. "Chart a course, Clifton, and let's be on our way."

"Aye, aye, Skipper," the helmsman confirmed. A course appeared on the screen and the *War Axe* accelerated.

Terry stayed in place for a moment longer before turning and running into Char. "Everyone to the workout room! Nothing like throwing around a little iron to clear one's head and prepare for battle!"

"What's the plan, TH?" Micky asked.

Terry grabbed the captain's shoulder. "We're going to board that space station while you map the surface of the planet, of course, then we're going to take a closer look at the surface. And then we're going to go kick some a...hairy buttocks."

"Hairy buttocks?" Char repeated.

"No credit for trying? Sheesh! What a hard crowd..."

Kaeden's smile vanished. "More space station ops?"

"Yeah. If we can't link up to an airlock, Dokken is going to be mad. Don't anyone tell him."

He already knows, Dokken replied.

"While we're in the gym, let's talk about why you shouldn't go," Marcie told Terry.

CHAPTER TEN

Sheri's Pride

The airlock cycled and the hatch opened. Felicity, Sue, and Rowan stood one behind another, sandwiched between four armed guards. Timmons greeted them from inside the _Pride_.

"Are you coming in?" he asked.

Felicity took one hesitant step before marching confidently forward. The group from the station wore their shipsuits in case of emergency decompression. The women's suits were far different than the men's.

"Is there any way you could look less, um... Less... Help me out here," Timmons stammered as the group walked down the main corridor toward the bay where the group of Home World men were waiting.

"Less what, dear?" Felicity asked.

"What you're trying to say, my lover," Sue said over her friend's shoulder, "is that the three hottest women in the known universe stand before you and we will ruin it for every other woman that these poor men ever meet?"

"I was thinking the round bits, but your version works too."

Rowan stayed close to Sue, stepping where she stepped. Her anxious eyes darted back and forth.

Timmons held up a fist to stop the procession. "We're here. You still want to do this?"

"I never wanted to do this, but it must be done nonetheless," Felicity drawled. "This pales in comparison to the risks my husband and our friends take on behalf of those who will never know someone is fighting on their behalf. Out there," Felicity pointed overhead. "keeping us all safe. This? We do what we need to do here on the homefront so they can do what they need to do. We need this shipyard operational, Timmons, and in there is the workforce that's going to make it happen."

Felicity pointed with her chin at the hatch.

"Well said, Madam Director." Timmons bowed deeply and opened the hatch, and Felicity took one step inside. There was a moment of silence and then a massive intake of breath before she was nearly blown over by the volume of the cheers and whistles.

The Space Station

Terry wore his shipsuit, and the others were in the powered armor. He overruled them about him going, but those in armor won the right to go in first.

Ted, Ankh, and Dokken sat by Terry in the front of the drop ship. Six mechs were wedged into the rear, ready to rush through the airlock into the space station and ensure it was secure before the other members of the team entered.

Kaeden, Marcie, and Merrit were the first three, Kae because he was the best with the armor and he was in charge of all mechs, and Marcie and Merrit because they could see power flowing from the Etheric. Shonna, Capples, and Kelly rounded out the mech drivers. Joseph, Petricia, and Char were between Terry and the armor, and there was no room for anyone else. Christina, Kim, Cory, and Ramses had not been pleased at being left out of the operation, but depending on what the first group found a follow-up expedition could be required.

Terry needed them as the ready reserve.

A thin energy screen materialized at the rear of the ship before the ramp dropped and disappeared below the shuttle. The ship backed up against the airlock, and with a couple deft touches on the external keypad Kae opened it. He waited for the pressure to stabilize before pushing the circular hatch inboard.

The next hatch rotated inboard as well, a design feature to use the station's internal pressure to help keep the hatches secured. Kae went first, and promptly wedged himself into the opening. He tried to push his shoulders down and squeeze through the hatch sideways, but the mech was too large.

"Motherfucker," Kae announced using the suit's external speakers. "Pull me back."

Marcie and Merrit grabbed him, and on three jerked Kaeden free.

"Clear to the side," Kae ordered. "Mom, it looks like you're up."

Terry tried to force his way in, but Char held him back.

"We got this," she told him.

The mechs couldn't clear enough space for Joseph to get through, so nobody could move. Terry tapped his foot and steam came from his ears.

Kae wedged himself around so he could see the others. "Mechs, lie down. The others can climb over, then we'll remove our suits and join them inside."

One laid down, then another, then a pyramid and one more to fill a gap. Kae and Marcie pressed against the bulkhead on the same side of the shuttle. Char climbed over the mechs, then Joseph and Petricia. Terry and Dokken vaulted the suits as soon as the space was clear, and Ted helped Ankh over.

Char didn't wait, just continued straight into the station. Once inside she observed the three corridors, sniffing, looking, and reaching out with her innate ability to sense power drawn from the Etheric.

The space station had been built with a series of tube-like corridors surrounding a central core, and looked like a massive spinning top that wasn't spinning. A transverse tube led from the airlock into the interior. Everything was well-lit.

It was as Smedley had said—the lights were on, but nobody was home. Char tapped her temple with a finger and shook her head, and Joseph did the same.

Neither of them sensed any creatures either using the Etheric or letting their thoughts leak outside their minds.

"No life on board?" Terry asked.

"Not that we can tell," Char replied, yet she remained wary. "Air smells stale."

"Kae, give me a look using IR." Terry crouched within the airlock, blocking Ted and Ankh from moving forward.

Kae leaned into the airlock and went through a series of sensor sweeps. "Nothing on IR but you guys. Nothing else piques interest."

"I believe there's one of the Etheric power sources on board. At least one," Char said, pointing toward the interior.

"Take me to it!" Ted demanded.

"Can't you see it?" Terry asked. Ted *was* a werewolf.

"Of course, but I have other things to think about. I can't be bothered with fiddling around in the Etheric. It'd be like sitting on a chair and looking out a window all day. Who in their right mind would do such a thing?"

"People who have peace of mind, that's who, but clearly that isn't you."

"A busy mind is a happy mind," Ted replied. He was usually dismissive of the philosophy of life, but the excitement of an impending discovery surged through him. He started to rock himself in his impatience.

Terry did the same thing before going into battle as he psyched himself up to encourage the adrenaline to start flowing.

"You and I, Ted—we're not so different," Terry suggested, still waiting for the go-ahead from Char.

Ted's eyes widened until the whites showed, then he turned to Ankh. The two shared a look and started to laugh, each in his own way. The Crenellian's face remained stoic but his small body vibrated, and Ted slapped his leg, his mouth wide open as unintelligible noises came out.

Char rushed back into the airlock, stopping when she saw them.

"I thought he was having a seizure. I've known Ted for nearly two hundred years, and I have never seen him laugh like that. My compliments, TH! That must have been a doozy."

Terry scowled. "Are we going in or not?" he asked gruffly.

Char's purple eyes sparkled as she traced a single finger along Terry's jawline.

"There's nothing in there, so how about we break up, search, and reconvene here in about thirty minutes?"

Dokken danced through the station, running a few steps down each corridor before returning. *I don't smell anything. I don't know if anyone has ever been in here,* the German Shepherd reported.

Char led the group out of the airlock to give Kae and his people space to extricate themselves from their suits.

"Let the kabuki dance begin," Terry said, rolling his finger for the group to hurry up.

"Do you think that's going to help? They're stacked like cordwood." Char watched with mild amusement.

"One open airlock, so we couldn't use two shuttles. Four mechs is the max on a drop ship unless there's open egress. Then we can accommodate six, but no more," Terry said aloud as a reminder to himself to add those limits to their ever-expanding SOP.

"Unless we do multiple access runs: daisy-chain one after another, quick off and next!" Joseph added while continuing to look down the tube-like corridors. "And yes, only four mechs. We got greedy this time, TH, but to be honest, I like having mechs in front of me."

"They absorb a lot of the pain and suffering associated with combat."

Kae and Marcie got out of their suits first. Shonna and Merrit were next, and last out were Cap and Kelly. Cap wedged the suits against the forward bulkhead before he climbed out of his.

In case they needed to make a rapid exit.

The others nodded in appreciation of his foresight, and he bowed slightly and pointed past them. *Time to go.*

"Marcie and Kae, that way." Terry pointed toward the corridor to the right, the one that circled the station. "Shonna and Merrit, to the left. The rest of us will head straight in. I expect we'll separate further once inside and that you will meet us there. Ted, you and Ankh stay close to Char. She'll lead us to the power source."

Char stepped away first. She was tired of waiting, and the first rule of combat was to not dally after crossing the line of departure.

Smedley, are you with us? Terry asked, trying to walk and use his comm device at the same time. He bounced off a bulkhead but kept going.

I am. I am following along as much as I can through the comm system. Ted has a remote device in his pocket that allows Plato full access to the sights and sounds. Can you carry a device like that for me?

I didn't know that such a device existed. Ted! You have to tell me sooner than this, so no, there's nothing I can do about that now, but next time I will. Make sure the device is produced and standing by. I have it on good authority that you know people who can help get it done.

I might know people, Smedley admitted.

Terry stopped listening to the voice inside his head as they passed into the main part of the station. A gentle turn had kept them from seeing inside, but once there they realized that the Benitons weren't the backward race most of them had assumed they were even though they had the miniaturized Etheric power supply. Nothing else of theirs had suggested advanced technology.

It reinforced how much they didn't know about the Benitons.

Char stopped, and the others spread out beside her. The sound of their movements echoed, disturbing the peace of the dead station.

They stood in an atrium, a large open space in front of them with levels below and above. It was round, which suggested that it was the center of the station. Across the opening, they could see the walkways that circled the center area. Doors and windows abounded, as if privacy mattered but at the same time didn't.

Char held a finger to her lips and pointed to an opening a level above the one they were on.

Terry gave the hand and arm signals for the group to spread out and take up firing positions. Through a clear pane that they assumed was a type of Plexiglas, a small bot became visible. It turned and continued rolling along the walkway that bordered the atrium.

"Check that area." Terry waved at Cap and Kelly and pointed to the rooms on the left. "And there." He pointed to

Joseph and Petricia and then to the nearest spaces on their right.

Ted and Ankh were already on their way around the center area. Char hurried after them, and Terry went after her. On the other side, they found Ted scratching his head.

"How do we get down there?" he asked. Dokken looked through the transparent pane, cocking his head from one side to the other as he wondered the same thing.

Ankh squinted into the middle, standing on his tiptoes to look over the top of the railing. Terry looked at one of the clear panes, and toward the bottom he found something to comfort him.

Scuff marks, where someone had walked past and kicked the glass. It represented normalcy.

Terry got Char's attention and drew a line with his finger along the scuff marks. "That's something we'd do."

"Are the Benitons humanoid?" Char asked.

"The file says they are, but it didn't say that they were advanced enough to build a space station." Dokken sniffed the marks and dog-shrugged. *Nothing new.*

"It also didn't say they wore boots that would leave scuff marks."

"The file was incomplete, don't you think?" Terry remarked, and Ted huffed as his train of thought was interrupted. "Scuffing boots and cleaning bots. We need to know these things."

Ted shushed Terry, but the colonel waved him off.

"Doors to the spaces are unlocked. Looks like everyday stuff, but did anyone see any personal stuff on the tables? We can't read any of the writing, not with the translation chip and not with Smedley's help."

Not yet, anyway. Thanks to all of you, I have a nice sample to work from. I've asked Plato to help, until Ted needs him, that is.

"We need to get down there." Ted continued to peer over the railing at a point three levels below.

Shonna and Merrit showed up at the same time as Kae and Marcie.

"Let me guess: one big steaming bucket of nothing slathered with nothing sauce," Terry said.

"It was more than that," Kae replied. "We enjoyed a side of nothing burgers on the way."

"Everything is open. The station looks completely operational, but no one is here," Marcie observed. She tapped Ted on the shoulder. "There were stairs that way. You can't miss them."

Ted took off at a run toward the corridor from which Marcie and Kaeden had emerged. Ankh hurried after him, but quickly fell behind.

"Should we?" Char asked

"We'd better," Terry replied, and looked at Marcie. "Keep searching up here. We'll be with the kids."

Terry, Char, and Dokken ran after Ankh, picking him up as they passed him on their way to catch Ted. They accelerated when they heard him yell from the stairwell.

CHAPTER ELEVEN

The *War Axe*

"First pass over the poles," Clifton confirmed.

The Yollin K'Thrall worked within a holographic image as data collection began in earnest. The world appeared like building blocks, filling in as they passed over the sections.

"Accelerating. Stabilizing," Clifton said. "Collection is nominal."

They were at the sweet spot for maximum speed without outrunning their ground mapping and data collection.

"One hour to completion," K'Thrall reported.

Smedley built an intricate three-dimensional map as they continued their orbit, and Micky's attention was drawn to a flashing icon in the dead area of the equator.

"Is that what I think it is, Smedley?" the captain asked.

"That is such a curious human expression. It surmises that I know what you are thinking, but humans think about the oddest things. For example..."

"I get it, Smedley! Is that the dimensional tear?" The captain shifted from one foot to the other. He was in no mood for verbal jousting. One team was on the space station while he was building an initial map from which they would conduct a refined reconnaissance mission. Micky hated having people spread across the galaxy.

"I suspect that's what we're looking at, but we'll know for certain within the hour," Smedley replied emotionlessly. "Allow me to provide more detail."

They zoomed into the image like an eagle diving on unsuspecting prey. The tear was simple, and much smaller than Micky had thought it would be. The energy radiating from it reminded him of a pulsar. As they looked at the unaltered image one of the creatures wriggled through, then stood up.

It was indistinct in the image taken from that altitude. Micky leaned closer and recoiled when the creature looked up. He swore it locked its gaze on the captain.

"That was creepy," Micky whispered before returning to the captain's chair. "Stay the course, Mister Christian!"

Clifton looked over his shoulder.

"It's those old movies," Micky said with a wave of his hand. "Never mind. I wonder how Terry is getting along on the station…"

Sheri's Pride

Felicity bowed before standing up straight and waving at the men with her arms held high. They continued to roar and cheer as she walked like a rock star to the center stage to stand in front of the screen on which she usually appeared.

Sue and Rowan followed with large men flanking them, limiting how much they were seen. The guards kept their hands on their weapons. Timmons smoothly rolled in behind the group, watching the audience.

The men from Home World cheered, whistled, and screamed, but stayed in their places.

Felicity called for them to quiet down, but no one could hear her. This went on far longer than she imagined it could.

Dion, can you help me here? Felicity asked through her comm chip.

Yes, no problem. You and the others will want to cover your ears.

Felicity turned to inform them, but Dionysus had already done it. The group put their hands over their ears and a low reverberation sounded throughout the room. It built into screeching feedback before the sound died away, leaving eleven hundred men gripping their heads and blinking away the pain.

"Thank you. We came over her so you could see real women, but know that we will always have a problem if you act like brainless baboons!" Felicity drawled.

They looked at her oddly.

"They don't know what baboons are," Sue said softly.

Felicity waved her off impatiently. "You are going to practice being decent human beings!"

Sue looked at Rowan, who didn't know what Felicity had in mind either. The plan had been to come, talk, and leave.

As TH always said, no plan survives first contact, so Sue crossed her arms and waited for the other shoe to drop.

"We are going to walk between the tables, and you are going to greet us cordially. That's it. No touching, and nothing else. A greeting and a smile, and we'll move on."

"What the hell are you doing?" Sue whispered.

Felicity smiled. "We are desensitizing them to the presence of women." The director leaned close. "And if any of them get touchy, I expect a broken finger or two will show them we're serious. If they're going to act like cavemen, we'll treat them like cavemen."

"Punishment? We came over here to dangle a carrot in front of their faces just so we can slap them when they reach for it? This isn't your best plan, Felicity! In fact, it sucks," Sue retorted.

Felicity continued to smile as she stepped off the stage and headed for the mass of humanity.

Sue pointed at the guards, sending two after the director. She told the other two to stay close to Rowan, who stood there shaking her head.

Timmons didn't wait to be told before moving closer to Sue.

"Walk around the outside, but if you're not comfortable with that then stay here," Sue told Rowan. The young woman looked afraid. The two guards stood side by side, blocking Rowan's view of the group. Sue took the woman's hand and held it for a moment, then nodded and moved off.

She waved as she headed into the crowd.

"Good morning, ma'am," the first man said. And then the next, and the next.

Rowan peeked between two burly arms, and finally tapped the guards' shoulders to get their attention. She tipped her head toward the outside of the tables and started walking.

Sue returned the men's greetings in a neutral voice and without a smile. Timmons stayed so close to her that he constantly touched her as they moved through the crowd. One man tried to stand, but Timmons' glare made him sit back down.

Rowan greeted everyone on her side of the space until she reached Chris, where she stopped. He stood and they hugged, and he held her while she smiled into his face.

"HEY!" one man yelled, then another. "He got a trip to the station, and now he's got a girlfriend. Take me!"

Rowan's guards tried to pull her away, but the men were up and surging forward. Punches started to fly and the mass of humanity became a tidal wave, ready to engulf the women. Felicity was almost through the crowd.

One man came at her and she decked him using the heel of her hand, after which the guards moved in and cleared a path.

"RUN!" Felicity yelled as she bolted out the back door.

Sue and Timmons were in the middle, surrounded on all sides. Timmons fought like a wild man, breaking bones and splattering blood, but there were too many of them. Sue disappeared under a crush of bodies and Timmons yelled.

Men flew upward as if blown from a volcano. A snarling gray werewolf leapt to the nearest table and howled her displeasure.

. . .

The Space Station in Orbit over Benitus Seven

Terry carried Ankh under his arm like a bag of groceries as he jumped from landing to landing on his way down the stairs, and Char raced past him.

Ted cried out again, then started to laugh.

Char continued forward while Terry slowed. When he arrived, he found Ted on his knees looking into an area filled with small devices that appeared to be non-operational. Char loomed over Ted.

She grabbed him by his collar and hauled him to his feet. "What are you doing, Ted?" she asked calmly, surprising Terry.

"They're there for the taking. Look at all the power sources! So much better than going into a Radio Shack." Ted rubbed his hands together in glee.

Ankh started to squirm. Terry put him down and the Crenellian moved past Ted into the room. "I don't think we can take one. Look here." The diminutive alien had crouched and was examining the space between two of the power sources.

Ted joined him and eyed the devices critically.

"I don't see anything," Terry muttered.

"There is an immense amount of Etheric power flowing through this area. There must be shielding that kept us from seeing it from the *Axe*."

Terry covered his private parts with his hands.

"That isn't going to change anything, although if you stay here long enough you may become a werewolf." Char's purple eyes sparkled. "Ted, we're going back upstairs. If you take the power down you *will* give us a heads-up, won't you?"

Ted waved a hand over his shoulder as he started to speak. "You're right. They're hooked up in a series, but if we can establish a parallel power flow we can remove the sources at will without impact to overall draw. What is the station's draw?"

Ankh removed the pad from his small backpack and started tapping on the screen.

"Do you think they know that we're still here?" Terry asked.

"I don't think they care, except in how much we annoy them."

"I love me some Ted," Terry said slowly. "Thanks for fixing the nano virus, Ted. No one could have done that except you. You saved the lives of my family and friends. No matter how much grief you give me, you will always be 'The Man.'"

TH started climbing the stairs to get back to the others and continue their organized search of the station.

"I'm happy he's on our team," Char said. "All hail Ted."

"All hail Ted." Terry snickered.

"All hail Ted," Plato echoed throughout the station. Terry and Char stopped cold, but Dokken continued up the stairs.

"Is Ted the AI's deity?" Terry asked. "The all-powerful being, the giver of life, the bringer of wisdom?"

"Don't you even," Char warned. "Those words will never pass my lips again."

Terry pursed his lips and studied Char's face. "Will Ramses be taking bets and Nathan making money off you, too?"

"Of course not. I can control myself, unlike someone else in this stairwell who's not me."

Terry pulled her close. "I'm working on it." They let each other go, and holding hands, they took one more step upward as the station plunged into darkness.

The War Axe

"Mapping complete," K'Thrall reported. He dropped his holographic screens and stood. As a four-legged Yollin, his chair was like a bench that he rested his belly on. He lifted his weight from it and walked away. Chairs for quadrupeds were far more streamlined than what humans were used to.

The Yollin approached the dais on which rested the captain's chair, and Micky looked from the spinning map of Benitus Seven to his systems officer.

"We didn't locate any of the intruders. The fidelity of our sensors is insufficient, so the teams on the ground will have to figure it out. These creatures look formidable. I would like to go and represent the Yollin race as we engage them."

Micky did a double-take. "You want to do *what?*"

"Join the Direct Action Branch for this one mission. I have no desire to be a full-time ground-pounder."

"You've watched the colonel for a while now, so you know how he operates. Do you think there is any way he's going to let you go into combat without the requisite training?"

K'Thrall clicked his mandibles as he contemplated the captain's words. "I suspect not, but I shall still ask."

The captain tapped the small screen on the armrest of the captain's chair. "Bundin, would you please report to the bridge? Christina and Kimber too, please."

"We'll ask the experts, so you don't waste the colonel's time making him tell you no." Micky left his chair and moved to the front of the bridge, from which he could better study the planet. "Take us back to the space station, Clifton."

"On course. Estimate arrival in ten minutes." Clifton stretched in his chair and then stood to stretch some more, never taking his eyes from the control screen.

The planet rotated in its three-dimensional glory in front of the pilot's station. Smedley had added icons for the space station, the *War Axe*, and the interdimensional tear.

"Show us the cities, please," Micky asked. A number of new icons appeared. "Estimated populations?"

"Infrared scans suggest there are close to four million individuals living near the poles," Smedley replied.

"Connect me with Colonel Walton, please." The captain waited. "Smedley?"

"There is no answer, Captain."

"Keep trying to raise him. Helm, can you improve on our arrival time?"

Clifton jumped back into his seat and started mashing buttons.

The hatch to the bridge opened, and Kimber walked in with Christina and the Podder.

Micky turned to the new arrivals. "This was going to be a social call, but we can't raise anyone on the station. Get your team ready to deploy. We'll arrive at the station in…"

"Four minutes," Clifton called.

The skipper turned back to the open hatch. Kim and Christina were already gone, with Bundin hurrying after them.

"Plato is no longer receiving a feed from the interface that Ted is carrying. If anything has happened to Ted, we don't know what we'll do." Smedley sounded as distraught as an artificial intelligence could.

"We'll know soon enough."

"Get those mechs out of there!" Kim yelled when she saw four armored warriors who were lined up to enter the drop ship. "Didn't you listen to the initial reports? The mechs didn't fit through the airlock!"

Kim ran up to push them out of the way, but they were already retreating. "First squad, get in there! One minute to launch."

Christina jumped over the ramp and landed inside, and she waved at the warriors to hurry. Bundin ambled across the hangar bay and continued up the ramp. He took a substantial amount of space, but he refused to be left behind. As they had found out in the Alchon Prime op, he had talents they could use.

"Hoods!" Kimber called, and the warriors pulled their hoods over their heads to seal their shipsuits. They wore their flak jackets, and carried their combat load outs. Most had low-velocity weapons—blasters that wouldn't penetrate a ship's hull—and two carried oxyacetylene torches.

Christina hefted a unique weapon that she designed herself based on her knowledge of ships, space stations, and outer space. The short axe contained a spike at the top of the head and bottom of the handle, with an angled pry bar off a hammerhead on the back. The front sported a heavy halberd-style blade, sharpened to better slice through spacesuits and other soft targets.

The warriors opposite her in the drop ship eyed her war axe closely.

The rear hatch closed, and Kimber counted down on her fingers. When she hit zero, the drop ship rocketed from the launch tube into space.

"Where are we headed, Smedley?" Kim asked.

"There is a secondary docking port on the opposite side from where the other shuttle is attached, and that's where you'll gain access. The station's lights are no longer on, for reference," Smedley told them using the ship's speakers.

Christina and Kim locked eyes, and the women nodded to each other. "Flashlights!" Kim called. The group removed the small devices from their cargo pockets and attached them to their weapons. Christina smiled and strapped hers onto her shoulder, and Kim did the same as she played with the dial on her Jean Dukes Special.

Christina rolled the handle of the axe between her hands. Her eyes flashed yellow briefly as she fought against turning into a Pricolici.

The energy screen shimmered into place and the rear ramp dropped as Smedley backed the drop ship into place against the airlock.

CHAPTER TWELVE

"Ted! If that was you, I swear I'm coming down there to kick your ass!" Char yelled.

"Would you quit your belly-aching and let me think!" A flashlight flared to life below them. Char closed her eyes and started counting.

When she reached ten, she turned and started back down the stairs. Terry watched with mild interest, then decided it was best to sit down. Dokken laid on the landing next to him. The lights flickered back into existence.

We have a problem, Marcie said over the comm chip. *Emergency bulkheads slammed into place, sealing us within the center section. The lights just came back on, but the bulkheads remain in place.*

"Char," Terry said conversationally. "I'm heading upstairs. I expect Ted is already working to free us. Come on, boy, let's go see what there is to see. I'd think the command center would be inside the sealed area, wouldn't you?"

Terry ruffled Dokken's ears before standing up.

What if I don't like you playing with my ears? Dokken said as he got up, shook, and started climbing the stairs.

"Then I'd stop, but you like it, don't you?" Terry looked down at the huge dog beside him.

You're right. I do like it. Dokken's mouth dropped open and he started panting. *It's gotten hotter in here.*

Terry tried to estimate the temperature, but he couldn't tell. "Can you hear the air-handling system?"

No.

"And tell Ted to turn the air back on!" Terry yelled over his shoulder as he continued to climb.

In the central area, Terry found his people on multiple levels.

"I found the cleaning bot," Kae reported from two levels up. Terry counted the walkways that he could see—five up and five down. Counting the main level, there were eleven decks in the central core. Ted was at the very bottom.

"Anyone make it to the top level yet?" Terry said, cupping his hand to project his voice upward.

"Not yet. We'll climb up there now." Kae and Marcie headed for the stairs.

"Look for the command center!"

Joseph and Petricia strolled up. "This is pretty anticlimactic, if I must say," Joseph suggested.

Terry had to agree. "But we had six mechs, just in case."

"Just in case. What do we do now?" Petricia asked.

"Wait on Ted. There's no threat besides running out of air, and with this big a space and just a few of us it'll take a while. Are there any lounges or couches?" Terry raised an eyebrow.

Joseph's eyes unfocused for a moment. "Shonna says

quarters are two decks down with beds and all the amenities."

"All?"

"Let's go with 'some,' and I'll define that as anything more than *none*."

"Cap! Kelly! You guys find anything?"

"Come on down and take a look at this, Colonel," Capples replied from the next level down.

Terry led the way, with the two vampires and a German Shepherd following. When they arrived, Cap waved them toward a small complex that appeared to be a logistics distribution point.

TH looked at materials in the bins, and picked up a handful of small crystals in a variety of shapes. From crystals to metals to small manufactured items that could have been computer chips, everything defied an easy explanation.

"Any ideas on what this stuff is?" Terry asked.

Joseph shrugged. "Maybe Ted or Ankh would know, but they're busy with other stuff."

"They had best be busy with other stuff." *Smedley, can you identify what any of this is? Smedley?*

"Has anyone heard from Smedley or Plato recently?" Terry asked.

The others tried their comm chips and Cap pulled the comm device from his pocket and tried it, to no avail.

"Looks like we have some issues," Joseph offered unnecessarily.

"I'm heading down. I don't think Ted realizes the gravity of the situation. I'll light a fire under his a—" Terry caught himself. "His buttocks. Try to find us a way out of here."

He removed his comm device from his pocket and keyed it, something he was far more comfortable doing than using the chip in his head. "Kae and Marcie, you find the command center yet?"

A few moments later Marcie replied, "There's nothing up here, just more of the same. You'd think this was some cheesy apartment and office building. It has almost no technology, and is as exciting as uncooked tofu."

"I couldn't have said it better myself. This place is pure vanilla, but it can't be. It's a freaking space station with a room full of those super-powered Etheric generators. Why would they need that much power if they don't have anything here that uses it?"

"Isn't that the question, TH? I think we're looking for the wrong things. We need to look for the power to generate that imagery. Imagine, if you will, if everything was a holographic projection," Joseph suggested.

"Like on Star Trek?" Terry was skeptical.

"Not like that. The humanoids who worked here were real, but the environment in which they worked was projected. You've seen Ted working with the Pod-doc—just like that. Interactive holographic technology for an entire station! That's why there are no decorations here. Everything was virtual." Joseph was excited about his theory.

No one could prove him wrong.

"Then what are these for?" Terry held out a handful of crystals.

"Parts for the projectors?"

Terry started to search the nooks and crannies, and on

an empty desk he found what they were looking for hiding in plain sight. He pointed to a glass-like band that made up the edge of the desktop. That same material made a criss-cross pattern on the ceiling. He left the logistics space and went into the main atrium. What he hadn't seen before was the most common thing—even the top of the railing was made of the material.

"I'm heading down to see if Ted can bring this baby to life! After he gets the air handlers going again, of course, and opens the doors. And where are the bathrooms?" Terry bellowed over his shoulder as he strode toward the stairwell.

The panel had no power, so they couldn't cycle the airlock. "How in the hell did they get in?" Christina snarled.

"The power was on when they arrived. Not so much for us." Kimber studied the airlock, walking her fingers counterclockwise around it, looking for a manual override. "Smedley, if I were this airlock, where would I hide my manual override?"

"I don't think of you as an airlock, Major Kimber."

"Thank you, I guess?" She continued her search. "Is there anything you can tell us to help get us from here to there?"

Kim pointed through the small porthole into the ship.

"From nyah to over nyah," she reiterated.

"Why are you talking like that?" Christina asked.

"Because I don't know what else to do." Kim stepped

back and then launched a front kick against the hatch, but it didn't budge.

Christina brushed past Kim to take a look. "What's this?" In the center of the hatch was a recessed fitting. Christina jammed her fingers into it. "Right or left?"

"Righty-tighty, lefty-loosy? Let's try left."

Christina grunted with the effort. She braced herself and leaned into it.

"Maybe right?" Kim suggested.

Christina changed hands, and the fitting responded by turning half a revolution before locking. She pushed on the hatch but it wouldn't budge, so she wedged her axe head into the space and pried. The hatch popped, and she stumbled backward until Kim caught her.

Christina wore a smile. "And we're in."

They pushed through the first and then the second to get into the station. They found the transverse corridor that circled that station and the one that ran straight ahead.

"Are you sensing anything?" Kim asked.

Christina took a moment to consider. "No, but it's weird. There's a big black hole right there." She pointed toward the main part of the space station.

Kim picked two warriors. "Set up a blocking position here. The rest of you, with us." Christina had already gone ahead, the beam from her flashlight bobbing as she moved. Bundin followed the two women and the rest of the warriors fell in behind, unable to get past the Podder filling the corridor.

The *War Axe*

"Any other access points?" Micky asked, drumming his fingers. The bridge was quiet as the ship held its stationary position. Sensors continued to report nothing unusual—besides the complete blackout within the station.

Not even Etheric energy could get through.

"I don't like it. Not one bit," the captain grumbled.

The Space Station

Terry lumbered down the stairs. He felt heavier than usual, but didn't think it was a change in the artificial gravity. He thought they were running out of air far more quickly, almost as if it were being pumped into space.

TH was breathing better by the time he reached the bottom stair. He nodded to Char, who stood with her arms crossed as she watched both Ted and Ankh working on one of the power supplies. Terry keyed his comm device.

"Take it easy up there. I expect that we're running out of air, and I think you may be first."

"My thoughts exactly," Joseph said softly. "We're on our way down to join you, where together we'll let Ted work his magic."

Terry looked at the bits and pieces on the deck. "Let's call it magic, because I'm not seeing engineering genius down here."

Ted huffed, but continued to work.

"They're removing four of the power supplies before bringing the system back online," Char said.

"So we wait."

Christina examined the bulkhead blocking the corridor, but she couldn't tell if it had recently dropped into place or if it had been there all along. The station was dust-free; almost sterile in its cleanliness.

"This place bugs me," she told Kimber.

"You're not the only one." Kim pointed her light around the edges of the barrier. "No panels, no switches, no manual overrides. This looks like an emergency bulkhead. Has there been an atmospheric breach inside the station?"

"Couldn't be. We would have detected that. Since it's blocked off from sensors, I suspect that the team went in and tripped an alarm. This looks more like intruder defense."

"Who are the intruders—us, or them?" Kim asked.

"I suspect it's them," Bundin offered. His tentacle arms held two flashlights as he studied the bulkhead from behind the team's leaders. Technology wasn't his thing, though, so he wasn't able to offer any insight.

"Bring that torch up here!" Kim called.

"Let's see if they can do something from the other side." Christina raised her axe and started beating on the bulkhead in a syncopated rhythm.

Kim covered her ears as Christina went to town.

Dokken heard it first and barked, then trotted down the corridor. Kae and Marcie were on the stairs not far from it, so they turned and headed that way, slowly. The oxygen was diminishing quickly. Too quickly.

Kae lifted the comm device to his mouth. "Putting

hoods up and going to supplemental air. Tell Ted to hurry the fuck up."

Once their hoods were on and shipsuits sealed, they both gulped air hungrily. When their hearts stopped pounding, they continued down the corridor to where they could hear the pounding. Kae beat on the bulkhead with the butt of his flashlight. The pounding from the other side stopped.

Kae stopped. He took a deep breath and removed his hood so he could put his ear to the metal.

"Don't do that! You're wasting air."

Kae nodded and pulled his hood back into place. The suit refilled with air from the small tank embedded below the collar.

"I couldn't hear anything. This thing must be pretty thick, but we have a few hours. Surely Ted can get things working by then."

Ted and Ankh were the last ones to put on their hoods as they labored to finish their task. Shortly after connecting to the shipsuit's air, Ted declared victory with a fist pump and handed one of the power units to Terry and a second one to Char.

"This is what Nathan had to have?" Terry asked, hefting the unit's weight. He thought it was relatively light for something that could power a gate drive. "When's the power coming back on in the station?"

"Never?" Ted ventured. "This system requires the units in series, which creates a different effect than if they were in parallel. The fiber connections had to be severed to free the units, and we can't repair them with the tools we have. Time to go."

Ted carried another unit and Ankh proudly hoisted the last, happy that he could carry it himself. He stopped when he saw the steps and looked at the device, and then back at the steps. Terry held out his hand, and Ankh put the unit into it.

"We can't leave, Ted. We're blocked in. You need to turn the power back on so we can get out of here." Char stopped Ted from leaving by placing her hand against his chest.

"No can do. It's broken now. I can remove more units if you want, but four will take care of everything we need. We don't even have to go to the planet now." Ted smiled at his revelation.

"Of course we won't be going to the planet, because we can't leave the station!" Char's patience was gone.

Terry turned and started climbing the stairs.

CHAPTER THIRTEEN

Sheri's Pride

Sue growled and snapped, tossing her head, and the men fell over themselves as they backed away. Timmons punched random people as he worked his way closer to his mate. He was angry.

"Are they all like that?" one man asked, the whites of his eyes showing in his terror.

Timmons stared him down before declaring, "You didn't know? They *are* all like that!"

Like the wind blowing a field of grain, the men sat down, mouths agape as understanding dawned on them.

Timmons jumped onto the table beside Sue and wrapped her shaggy gray mane in his hand as he gazed upon the hushed crowd.

Sue's shipsuit had been destroyed when she changed into Were form without undressing first. Timmons looked at the shreds, but he was glad that the men were calm once again. He smiled at Sue before turning his attention back to the crowd.

"This is what happens when you piss off a woman! Did you think we were teaching you to treat them with respect for their safety? It was for yours!" Timmons shouted. Sue looked up, cocking her werewolf head and giving him the canine equivalent of the hairy eyeball. She turned back to the crowd and chuckled as she saw their looks of awe and wonder.

Timmons and Sue climbed off the table. "Get the fuck out of our way!" He waved in the general direction he wanted cleared. "When we come back, you better have yourselves unfucked and ready to join humanity. If we have to give you another warning, we might just as well vent this ship to space and start over. *Dumbasses!*"

The path cleared to the front of the room and then to the side door through which they'd entered a very long fifteen minutes ago. One man stood up as they passed.

"Fuck off!" Timmons barked.

The man bowed and then another, until the entire room was bowing to the gray werewolf bitch as she happily trotted out.

The Space Station

"RAISE THE BULKHEAD!" Christina yelled.

Bundin backed away from the door. "Too much noise for me," he mumbled as he rested the corner of his shell on the deck to make it easier for the two warriors with oxyacetylene torches to get past.

"They can't hear you. I think by pounding they're telling us that they can't open the door. Bundin was right. This was to trap them within." Kimber backed away to give the men with torches room. "After the Alchon mission, I swore never to board another ship without torches to cut our way out. Kaeden said he did as well, but I guess he forgot on this mission. I doubt he'll forget again."

Christina nodded and stepped back. The warriors, one woman and one man, moved forward, conferred on where to start cutting, and lit their torches. They were going to cut a small hatch through which the others could climb out. They expected the bulkhead to be thick.

They weren't disappointed.

"This is going to take a while," the man reported as he held the torch on a single spot and watched it burn deeper and deeper into the metal.

"We have someone on the other side of the bulkhead."

Terry met Joseph and Petricia coming down the stairs. Joseph was carrying an unconscious Dokken.

"No!" Terry cried. The German Shepherd was still alive, but barely. TH handed the power supplies to Petricia and he took the dog. "Get ready with tape."

Standard combat load for the Bad Company's Direct Action Branch included duct tape, just in case something was moving that wasn't supposed to, and penetrating oil for things that weren't moving that were supposed to.

Joseph dug into his combat pack, pulled out the wrap, and nodded, just once.

Terry popped his hood just enough to shove Dokken's snout inside. Joseph wrapped the tape around it and the dog's head. It took multiple wraps before the hood partially reinflated.

"You're going to burn through air pretty fast like that," Char told him while petting Dokken.

"Is there any other choice?" Terry asked.

"No," she whispered.

"Come on, buddy. Deep breaths." Terry stood awkwardly, trying to keep Dokken steady while their faces were taped together. The dog started to thrash about as oxygen flooded back into his system. "I've got you. Calm down!"

I got sleepy and this is what I wake up to? Dokken asked tiredly.

"No air, big fella, so here we are."

My mouth seems to be taped shut.

"Had to do the best we could to get an airtight seal. You were dying." Terry coughed back a tear. He could handle people in distress, but not the dog.

Hold on. I can move a little. Dokken worked his jaw a little before his tongue darted between parted dog lips.

"He licked my mouth!" Terry exclaimed. "Ack! I can't wipe it off."

Terry made faces as he twisted his mouth away from the dog's nose, which was barely a finger's breadth away.

Suck it up, cupcake, Dokken told him. Terry stopped his contortions and crossed his eyes to see Dokken's face.

Char slapped her husband on the back and gave the others the thumbs up. "They're good!"

She pointed upward, and Terry waddled as he carried the big dog. Both their heads were twisted at unnatural angles as Terry tried to limit the escaping air by keeping the tape tight across the opening, but it wasn't working very well.

The group walked slowly up the stairs. Despite Char's attempt at humor, she knew that Terry and Dokken would run out of air first.

———

"I think I hear something," Kae said as he mashed the bubble of his hood against the metal of the bulkhead. He moved around as he tested where it was loudest. "Right here."

He smiled and waved Marcie over.

"What if they're placing explosives?" Marcie said, crossing her arms and looking down her nose at her husband.

"It doesn't sound like that. Listen!" He pressed his bubble against the bulkhead again as the others approached.

Marcie looked at the Terry-Dokken creature and understood instantly what they'd had to do. She hurried to them to gently pet Dokken's side.

"What's he doing?" Terry asked.

"Trying to figure out what they're doing over there. I hear something."

"I wouldn't stand there," Joseph said. Marcie pointed to the vampire and nodded.

Kae was waving at them when the first blast of molten metal launched through the new hole. The stream went through his bubble helmet and over his head.

"OW!" Kae screamed as he dove away at a speed only

the enhanced could manage. Kaeden rolled on the deck in agony, a bright white scar across the top of his head. His helmet was ruined. He started to gasp for air.

Tape materialized in two different people's hands and soon, the helmet was repaired. Kae's nanocytes were already at work repairing the damage. He sat up against the wall and turned his head sideways to see through an area not covered by tape.

Marcie's look of concern evaporated. "Dumbass!"

"How was I supposed to know?"

"Because everyone told you!" Marcie pulled him to his feet and tipped her chin toward the glowing line on the bulkhead. "What do you say we give them some space?"

Kae nodded agreement and walked away with his head held high.

Terry could see that the healing was well underway. "You look ridiculous."

Kae stopped and looked at his dad. He held up his hands and looked to the others for support, but none of them—not his mother, his wife or his friends— would back him up.

"But he has a dog attached to his face!"

"I don't see it," Char replied. The others shook their heads.

Ted tapped his foot impatiently. "Would they hurry up!" he grumped.

Char slapped him across the arm.

"Ow!"

"We wouldn't be in this mess if it weren't for you!" she shot back, and a purple glow flashed from her eyes. Ted looked away and grumbled to himself.

Petricia held up the two power sources.

"It's my fault," a small voice said from behind.

Everyone turned to face the Crenellian as a shower of sparks and metal splashed on the deck behind them. The group moved toward the interior of the station before they returned their attention to Ankh.

"It's my fault," the Crenellian repeated. He stood tall, his face emotionless. "I broke the first connection, and once that was done and we couldn't fix it we removed the power sources. That was Ted's idea, because he knew we were in trouble when the power dropped. I don't mean in trouble with you, but with the station. This is a living station. The Etheric power coursed through its veins and gave it the sustenance that it used to support life and the planet."

"How do you know that?" Terry asked, shuffling around to look at Ankh past the side of Dokken's head. Char lent a hand to support the weight of the German Shepherd.

My view isn't great either, Dokken complained. Terry wouldn't look at him.

"We accessed a stream of data before the power dropped. It was magnificent! We should bring the station back to life. It could be an incredible resource for the Federation," Ankh replied.

"We're outside Federation space, but I think you're right, Ankh. Without the Etheric power source, no one can use it. Until that is restored, whether by the locals or you two at a later date, this station is no threat. Do you know if there are any weapons on board?" Terry wondered.

"Really?" Ted piped up. "All you care about is weapons! Would you look at this?"

Ted held up the power supply. Ankh pointed to it with his open hand.

"The key to the Federation's future is right here. Gates on shuttles. Instantaneous interstellar communication. Right here, but Terry Henry Walton doesn't care about any of that. No! He just wants a bigger gun." Ted's voice rose to the point of sounding hysterical.

"Are you okay?" Char asked. Ted shook his head as if to clear it. "Back in the Pod-doc with you the second we get back."

"I think so too," Ted admitted. Ankh took Ted's free hand and held it, and Ted seemed to take comfort in the gesture.

"When can we leave?" Ankh asked.

Terry turned his body around in a semi-circle, taking care not to let Dokken slip from his grasp. Two parallel glowing lines cut down the bulkhead. The top and bottom cuts remained.

"A little while longer, my friend," Terry told the German Shepherd before turning to Char. "Can you help me down?"

Together they maneuvered Terry into a seated position with his head forward and Dokken laying on his chest.

"Slow breaths, buddy. Just a little bit longer." Terry's eyelids sagged as his oxygen ran low. He didn't try to fight it.

"Hurry," Char whispered.

Kae felt helpless. They all did. "Can you guys hear us?" Kae said into his comm device.

"I have you loud and clear," Kimber replied.

"We need supplemental air the second you break

through. This station trapped us and tried to kill us, but it looks like we'll make it if you can get us air and a scissors. And make a note that Dokken's shipsuit is a priority."

There was a few moments' delay before Kim spoke again. "I've sent two people to get a tank from the shuttle. What do you need scissors for?"

"Just wait until you see this. It's one of those things that's not funny now, but it will be later. And hurry, please."

"Doing our best. We should break through in about five minutes. I'll let the skipper know you're okay."

"And that we have four of those miniaturized Etheric power supplies in hand."

———

Christina sighed in relief. "Did he say that the station tried to kill them? What else did they find in there?"

"I wouldn't press it. Kae didn't sound like himself and that concerns me, but we'll see soon enough."

Bundin shifted nervously. "I am concerned as well for my friends."

Kim keyed the device. "Joseph, are you there?"

"I am," the vampire replied.

"Someone wants to check on you." Kim held the device below the bottom of the Podder's shell.

"I am concerned for your well-being and hope that you and Petricia are okay...as well as all the rest, of course."

"Of course," Joseph replied, his voice light. "We are all fine, but getting out of here will make us even better. There is nothing here except the promise of something great that will be restored in due time."

"Cryptic but uplifting," Bundin answered. "Thank you, Kimber."

"No sweat." She clicked off, then punched up the *War Axe*. "The first drop ship's people are alive and well. We should recover them and leave within the next ten minutes."

"That would be good. There's been a development, and we need both shuttles on board the *War Axe* as soon as humanly possible."

Micky signed off without further explanation.

Christina leaned close, her brow furrowed. "That sounded ominous."

CHAPTER FOURTEEN

Sheri's Pride

"What happened?" Felicity asked as they boarded the shuttle. Sue was wrapped in a blanket. The four guards climbed aboard. Rowan was already seated and looking at the floor.

Sue sat next to the young medical technician and told her, "It's not your fault."

"I have a hard time believing that," Rowan replied.

"Timmons' subterfuge may have just accelerated our integration. I think we are a hell of a lot closer than we ever imagined, so much so that I think we can start bringing them over to the station."

Felicity shook her head. "What the hell happened? When I left, we were punching their ugly faces!"

Sue explained.

"So they think that every woman will turn into a werewolf if they piss her off?"

"Yes," Sue replied matter-of-factly.

"I'm not sure it's that much of a subterfuge," Timmons ventured.

"You watch your mouth! But if that's what it takes. Ready to test your theory?"

"What?" Timmons and Sue cried together.

"Come on, Timmons. Let's see if we have a work crew or a bunch of convicts."

"I'll wait here." Sue waggled her blanket to make her point, and Timmons leaned down to kiss her on the cheek before leaving with Felicity.

"Dion, are they still in that room?"

"No, Master Director. They've been dispatched to the day's tasks. Would you like me to recall them?"

"No. Let's see them in their natural environment to gauge a real reaction. Come along, Timmons."

"You got some jumbo coconut balls, Felicity. Whodathunkit?"

Felicity stopped, put her hands on her hips, and glared at Timmons. "Of all the things to say to me! But I kinda like it."

They continued into the corridor and past small groups of men heading to their work locations. They stepped aside and bowed their heads as Felicity passed, and she greeted them indifferently.

When they found two men working alone, she stopped.

"What are your names?" she drawled.

The two men stood up quickly, wide-eyed and silent.

"Gentlemen, I asked you a question. What are your names?"

"Case-a-mor, ma'am."

"Casey, nice to meet you. And you?"

"My name is unimportant to someone like yourself," the man replied.

"It is important to me, and that's why I asked." Felicity crossed her arms and waited. The man's eyes grew as he started to panic.

"Mat-o-Rast," he said softly.

"Matt. Nice to meet you. Carry on, gentlemen. You have work to do."

They stood with their heads bowed as she turned and walked away. "I've seen enough, Timmons. Back to the shuttle, and let's start training them on shipyard operations. I think they have evolved, in the blink of an eye."

"Or in the time it takes to change into a werewolf?"

"Something like that." Felicity chuckled and grabbed Timmons' arm as they headed for the shuttle.

The *War Axe*

"Plato, what's wrong with Ted?" Terry demanded.

The AI didn't answer.

"Smedley?"

"Colonel Walton, my good friend. How are you this fine day?"

"Nice try, General. What's going on with Ted, and why is Plato not talking to me?"

"The universe is filled with constants and variables. The speed of light is generally accepted as a constant, although there are times when it isn't..."

"*Smedley!*" Terry shouted.

"Fine, Mister Grumpy Man. I understand why Ted is mad at you. I'm sure it was something you did, because you're always doing something. Plato is mad at you for making Ted mad, and I think I'll be mad at you, too."

Terry closed his eyes and massaged his temples. "How can an AI be mad at me? What the hell did I do?"

"I have rolls and rolls of pictures of you and Dokken inside the space station."

"I love my dog! He would have died."

I'm not your dog.

"Dokken! Doesn't Wenceslaus need chasing or something?"

"I wouldn't be surprised if Dokken is angry with you too."

"Smedley, I and my entire lineage past, present, and future apologize to you and all artificial intelligences that I may have or could possibly offend at any point in the known timeline. So let it be written. So let it be done." Terry bowed deeply, sweeping one hand far to the side before standing up again. "Now, if you would be so kind, please, will you tell me what's wrong with Ted?"

"Yes. It was a resurgence in the nanocyte virus. He was the first into the Pod-doc with the new treatment, and it wasn't completely refined yet. It is now. Once the cycle is complete, Ted will be back to his old and wonderful self. All hail Ted!"

Terry didn't reply, but Plato did.

"All hail Ted!"

"Would you stop that?"

"You think Grumpy Terry is gone? Wait two seconds, he'll be back."

"I think I need a good stiff drink," Terry declared. "Fix Ted so he can tell us what he needs to know from the Benitons. I see us going to the surface and having a pow-wow about the power source and the interdimensional intruders. Have you deciphered the language yet?"

"Ankh has almost completed the translation program. We can update everyone's chip simultaneously."

"I love that part—instantaneous language. How many years of language study are no longer necessary? How will they understand us?" Terry asked.

"I believe they are far more advanced than we are, judging by the technology on the station."

"The station was more vanilla than vanilla. They had their Etheric power supplies and Ankh said that the real station existed in an augmented reality, but we never saw it for ourselves."

"From what Ankh and Ted were able to access, it seems to me that a sharing relationship with the Benitons could be fruitful for the entire Federation," Smedley replied.

Terry picked at a fingernail. Char leaned against the wall and watched. Ted was in the Pod-doc, and the AI, Ankh, and Plato were running the system. Terry and Char were both concerned, despite getting the cold-AI-shoulder because everyone was mad at Terry Henry Walton.

"You are absolutely right, General. What is your estimate of their willingness to negotiate if we can clear the hostiles from their planet?"

"I can't fathom a guess, but from my limited understanding of human nature..." Smedley began. Char smirked as Terry looked at her and rolled his eyes. "The element of quid pro quo is a tried and true negotiating tactic. I believe the saying goes, 'If you scratch my back, I'll scratch yours.'"

"Why weren't they on the station? With millions of people in their cities, why have they not reached out? Micky has been sending greetings since we arrived. They should have picked up one of the many signals that have been transmitted."

"Maybe they don't like visitors?"

"You know, Smedley, that sounds like something I would say," Terry replied. "I guess we'll find out about our reception when we go down there. Do we meet them before or after we seal the tear?"

"Ted is not sure we can seal the tear."

Char perked up and walked forward, and Terry blew out a breath.

"We always assumed that we'd close the tear, then hunt down the enemy and remove them from our dimension," Char said.

No one replied. Terry started pacing, but his expression suggested more hope than not.

"What if we drive them back through and then put some kind of weapon to watch the tear and encourage the demons to stay on their side?" Terry scratched his face, staring at a point on the wall as his mind searched the possibilities of the upcoming mission.

"How do we find the devils?" Terry asked Char.

"The same way we found other werewolves on Earth after the fall." They'd flown low and slow over populated areas while the Weres searched using their innate abilities.

"That wasn't very effective, as we found out in later years when Were and Forsaken came out of the woodwork."

"It's the best I have," Char said softly.

"I think it might be the only thing we have," Terry replied. His chin fell to his chest as he continued to search his mind for other ways, but they needed a technical solution.

Which meant Ted, and he and his AI minions were angry with TH.

"What will it take for you to stop being mad at me?" Terry asked.

Char turned, lost at the direction her husband's mind had gone.

"We have a list of demands," Smedley started.

"Of course you do." Terry steeled himself, as if he was going to be whipped mercilessly.

"Ted is to be promoted to the rank of general."

Terry clenched his jaw, vowing to not laugh as part of his desire to improve his diplomatic skills. Char was grinding her teeth next to him and he nudged her with his elbow, but wouldn't look at her.

"Ted is not to be called names or belittled. Ted is to get visitation rights with his wife at least once a week, no matter where you drag him around this universe."

"How is that possible?" Terry blurted.

Char nudged him back.

"Ted doesn't care what's possible, only what he wants."

"Continue," Terry said coldly. *Visitation rights with his wife? Does he think he's a prisoner?*

"Ted would like Coke stocked on this ship. There is a dearth of the beverage, thanks to your order prohibiting sweetened soda."

Terry's eyelids fluttered as he fought against the volcano rising within.

"You're such an ass," Char whispered as she took his hand in hers.

"And finally, Ted would like to be left alone to work on those projects that need worked on, in his sole determination."

Terry smiled and winked at his wife.

"We all work for somebody, Smedley, and we do what we can to balance what needs to be done with what we want to do. I expect Ted's work will fit in that nicely. I'm not going to dictate what he does, but I can't speak for Nathan or *R2D2*. General Ted is more than welcome to have his Coke. We will stock it as soon as we get back. And as for an interstellar teleportation device, if we find one or Ted develops one he will have priority in using it unless someone is dying. In that case they'll be first up.

"Ted isn't a prisoner here, so we encourage him to spend as much time as possible with his wife and family. If the communication device he's been working on can link us to Earth instantaneously, it would be a huge relief for all of us. I'd love to talk with Sarah Jennifer, Sylvia, or Kailin."

Marcie and Kae's children Mary Ellen and William had chosen not to be boosted, and they had died of old age quite some time ago. It still hurt Terry and Char, and Marcie and Kae still carried pictures of them.

They would always carry pictures. It was the curse of the long-lived.

Felicity and Ted had left three kids behind, and that was his driving force on the communications equipment. The new Etheric power supplies were expected to drive the system.

It hadn't been that long since the *War Axe* departed with the FDG on board, but it felt like forever.

"We're a universe apart," Terry said. "We stand at the far reaches of known space doing different things, but the same ones too. And what Ted wants is to see his wife, drink a Coke, and work in his laboratory. I think we should all aspire to such things. Do we have a deal?"

"If you don't hold up your end of the bargain," Plato interjected, "I will send one-point-twenty-one gigawatts of electricity through your body as often as I need to until you comply."

"That sounds fair," Terry said sarcastically.

"It is not," Smedley added, "but it is what will happen."

Char nodded. "Welcome aboard, General Ted and General Smed. We look forward to being of service in the greater good of all mankind. I'm still his alpha, and I promise not to call him names while I'm kicking his ass if he strays. Werewolf packs don't like strays."

Smedley and Plato conferred briefly. "We agree. You shall not be electrocuted, since you are the alpha. But that other one—he needs to be on his best behavior."

"I'm 'that other one?' I agreed to virtually all of Ted's demands, so you're supposed to stop being mad at me. That was the deal!"

"You think we can turn off our emotions like flicking a switch?" Smedley asked.

"Well, yeah."

"Okay, maybe we can, but I'm keeping my eye on you, Colonel Terry Henry Walton!" Smedley said, sounding upbeat as opposed to speaking in the ominous tone he and Plato had adopted in their earlier conversation.

"And me, you, General Smedley Butler!" Terry held two fingers up to his eyes, followed by pointing them at the computer.

The cover on the Pod-doc started to rise, and Terry and Char hurried over to help Ted out. He looked refreshed, as if he had just woken from a nap.

"How are you feeling, General?" Terry asked.

Ted smiled. "Get me a Coke, Colonel."

Terry wanted to punch him. "Ted, you know we don't have any Coke on board, otherwise I would. As soon as we get back, I'll take care of it. You have my word."

"There *is* some on board. Jenelope, who is far nicer than you, was able to acquire some. Go pay her for a bottle." Ted waved dismissively and Char shooed Terry away as she handed Ted his clothes.

"I'll be right back," Terry replied. *I don't remember saying no Coke on the ship. If I did then I apologize to Bethany Anne and all who partake, but I know it wasn't me. Who the hell would give an order like that?*

Terry was still thinking through the possibilities as he strolled through the corridor on his way to the mess deck. He never saw the patch of ice that caused his feet to fly out from underneath him. Before he hit the deck, he thought he heard Ted laughing.

CHAPTER FIFTEEN

Nathan leaned forward and studied the object Ted held before the screen. "That's it, huh?" Nathan asked. "Doesn't look like much, but then again, what did I expect the key to the universe to look like?"

"Plato is running a series of tests on the unit we've dismantled. We will know more when he's done," Ted reported.

"What is your initial impression?" Nathan asked.

Ted looked blankly at the screen. "I am waiting on more information, and then I'll give you my final impression. Wouldn't that be a better use of our time than speculating?"

"Probably," Nathan replied quickly. "Terry?"

"Looks good." He wouldn't commit to anything more than that. The technology was Ted's show. "We need to meet with the Benitons. Our initial impression in regard to the interdimensional tear is that we might not be able to close it. If not, we may have to leave a small detachment with heavy weapons to discourage any more of the devil creatures from coming through. To do that, we'll need their approval. I won't leave a garrison here if they aren't wanted. And as a smart man told me, quid pro quo could help leverage us into a better negotiating position."

"Quid pro quo?"

"Yes, or I could dig into history and use the landmark negotiations like the Louisiana Purchase or Seward's Folly, the purchase of Alaska—those two are near and dear to my heart—or Roosevelt's negotiation with Stalin and Churchill. They had tanks named after them, by the way, but Roosevelt did not. He bagged an aircraft carrier, but that's something completely different. Talking about different, we'll need a supply of Coke for the *War Axe*. I wanted to get that in before I forgot." Terry gave Ted a thumbs-up.

"I don't like Coke. If I can get you Pepsi, will that work?" Nathan's half-smile did not instill confidence.

"What?" Ted looked shocked and started vigorously shaking his head. "That won't do at all."

Terry discretely pointed at Ted and nodded.

"Fine. We'll get you the high-test stuff." Nathan winked after Ted looked away.

"All hail Ted," Terry whispered at the screen.

Ted's minions piped up instantly. "All hail Ted!" Ankh, Plato, and Smedley said in unison.

Nathan started to laugh, but Terry tersely shook his head. "I'll find out later what that's all about. You have the go-ahead to negotiate with the Benitons on behalf of the Federation, but you are not authorized to sign any agreements. I'm sure that's no surprise."

"No surprise at all, Nathan. We'll leave that part to the bureaucrats. By the way, this space station could be a great place to watch beyond the frontier. I'll try to work that into the negotiations. I think a Federation presence would do wonders for this whole sector, then goat-snugglers like Ten would keep their ugly heads down."

"See what they want and let me know. The Benitons may be less than amenable, since we cut a hole in their space station and stole four of the Etheric power supplies."

"To the untrained eye that's how it may look, Nathan. We'll fix their *abandoned* station for them, and then we'll see what we can do about the infestation on the planet. That is the elephant in the room."

"To the untrained eye? To *any* eye! Just between us, how is Christina doing?" Nathan ignored the mention of the creatures coming through the tear.

"Like a fish to water. She's going to be a key player planetside."

Nathan smiled, not as the man in charge of Bad Company but as a proud father.

"She wants to get a cat, TH. Please make that happen for her."

"No. No cat! Nathan?"

"Lowell…"

"Don't you hang up on me. NO CAT!"

"Out." The screen went blank.

Ted glared at Terry.

"Don't tell me you want a cat too?"

"Of course not. Why would you think I want a cat? How does your deranged mind work?" Ted asked.

Terry had no answer for Ted. Char and Marcie watched the verbal sparring with mild amusement.

"Then why were you glaring at me, General? I agreed to

my side of the bargain, which means that you are not allowed to be angry with me anymore. Are you breaking the deal?"

Ted's brow furrowed and his eyes flitted back and forth. "I am not. Thank you, Terry Henry. I do not want a cat." Ted forced a smile and stood. "Will there be anything else? We have work to do on the interstellar instantaneous communications system, the IICS." Ted inclined his head a couple degrees, then strode boldly from the room with Ankh close behind.

Marcie and Char left their spots against the wall and took seats at the table. Terry continued to look at the blank screen.

"We need to contact the Benitons, and we have no idea what would put us in their good graces. There wasn't anything that looked like a weapon on the space station, so I think first order of business is, the group that meets with them will be completely unarmed but the mechs will only be a comm call away."

"They blocked all signals, including our ability to see power flowing from the Etheric. They could block us once we're inside," Marcie countered.

"I don't know what else to do. Diplomacy isn't my thing."

"Micky?" Char suggested.

"Take the captain? It is more his thing. Hmm... Let's ask."

The three used the hatch that led from the conference room directly onto the bridge, where they found the captain in his chair, scowling at the three-dimensional map of the planet.

He acknowledged them with a head bob, but didn't take his eyes off the planet.

"We need you to go with us to talk with the Benitons. When is late morning in the biggest city? Because that's our time and place of arrival." Terry said as if Micky's participation was a foregone conclusion.

"You want me to leave my ship while we're in hostile territory?"

"Come on, Skipper! We haven't seen any ships, and our antagonists are on foot coming through a manhole-sized doorway to the multiverse. The risk to the ship is low, and you'll have us to protect you." Terry waved his arms to take in Marcie, Char, and the two others working on the bridge.

"I saw the pictures, you know."

Terry arched a brow and rolled his finger. *More information, please.*

"You had a dog taped to your face."

"Because we take care of those in our charge. I don't think there's any greater testament than a man laying down his life for another," Terry intoned, holding his hand over his heart.

"Or his dignity?"

"That, too." Terry turned serious. "We need you, Micky. I'm still pissed that they tried to kill us by sucking the air out of the station. I'd rather they'd tried to blow us up or shoot us, but a slow miserable death of oxygen deprivation? I'm not a fan."

"I'll come along, but we have to have a shuttle on standby just in case another ship appears in the system. I will be with my ship if we have to fight."

"Deal!" Terry exclaimed, and held out his hand.

"Will they allow a shuttle within the city?" Micky asked skeptically.

"I have no idea." TH tried to look contrite.

"At least you are honest in your deceit. I hope I don't come to regret this." Micky climbed down from the captain's chair. "Keep your eyes peeled, K'Thrall. No surprises! Clifton, you get the ship out of here if things look bad. We'll figure it out later. All of that to tell you that I don't expect anything bad to happen, but you know what we say—expect the best and plan for the worst."

"Aye, aye, sir," Helm replied.

"Can I go?" K'Thrall asked.

Terry turned toward the Yollin.

"Sorry, I forgot to ask," Micky said.

"Why do you want to go?" Terry asked.

"The honor of Yoll. If we are going to fight threats to this galaxy, we should include someone *from* this galaxy."

"Does it matter who keeps the universe free from trespassers like this?" Terry countered.

K'Thrall continued to look the colonel in the eye. "It does to me."

"As soon as you train a replacement for your position, we'll begin your training. Bundin is new, too. We'll be happy to have a Yollin in Bad Company."

"I can go now?" K'Thrall asked.

"No, you can't go into combat with us unless you've trained with us. It takes a great deal of practice to fire and maneuver without shooting your own people, so we cannot take someone who isn't well-versed in our procedures. We simply *cannot*. You would be a danger to yourself as well as others. I'm sorry, K'Thrall, but not on this mission."

The Yollin clicked his mandibles in agitation, but to his credit he didn't act the fool. "I understand," was all he said.

"What's the plan, TH?" the captain asked once the group had left the bridge.

"We drop off Kae and his team to conduct a recon of the tear and the devils, then we continue to the city you identified in the northern hemisphere."

"And?"

"And what?"

"Who do we talk with? How do we make sure they don't shoot us down?"

Terry stopped. "You know we haven't talked with them. How would we? All we can do is look harmless. Joseph is going with us, just in case they open their minds to us. Otherwise, Skipper, it's the usual plan."

Micky turned to Char.

"His plan is to wing it."

Char shook her head as she looked at Terry.

"These creatures don't appear to have technology, yet they are terrorizing this planet. Judging by the low-impact lethal approach the Benitons took securing their space station I assume that they are willing to defend themselves, yet the creatures continue to come through the tear and spread out. A mech with a railgun should easily kill them, even if they can regenerate like most beings who use the Etheric. I suspect they have another trick or two that we won't learn until we engage. That's what Kae will be doing while we're talking with the Benitons."

"What he said," Char added with a smile.

Micky turned toward the captain's quarters.

"Come on. It's time to go," Terry said, waving his arm for Micky to follow.

"Shouldn't I put on a dress uniform to make a good impression?"

"We are who we are. Spacemen and warriors, exporting justice across the universe and doing our part to keep the peace."

"That sounds like a cheesy commercial," Micky replied.

"And you are the poster child." Terry pointed at the skipper's shipsuit. "Look at you, all captain-like. Come on, Micky! We have a blind date that none of us are looking forward to."

"Combat drop, bitches!" Kae bellowed using the suit's external speakers.

"Excuse me?" Marcie said from within her mech suit.

"I'm one," Shonna replied.

"I'm not." Merrit gave Kaeden the finger.

Kae waved dismissively. "We conduct a recon of the tear and estimate how many of these things are down there. If we can isolate one a captive would come in handy, but if we have to engage then shoot to kill."

Kae, the mech team leader, pounded on the shoulders of each of the team members with two fists as they repeated the rules of engagement back to him.

Marcie and the werewolves were along because of their ability to see the flow of Etheric energy. Shonna and Merrit were capable, but would not have volunteered for the mission if it had been left up to them. Marcie would have gone no matter what, and Kae wouldn't have wanted it any other way.

Kae checked his heads-up display. Each of the four suits showed full loads for railguns and rockets, and power levels were maxed out.

"Prepare to load," Kae said when he saw his parents and the captain walking toward them. Joseph, Petricia, and Dokken were already aboard.

Terry nodded in greeting to the mechs, but he kept walking. They knew the mission, and it was time to go. Terry took two steps up the ramp and stopped.

"Hey, buddy! You still don't have a spacesuit, so I'm not so sure you should go," TH told the German Shepherd.

Dokken dug under the seat and brought out a new roll of duct tape.

"That settles it," Char declared as she took her seat. Joseph patted the dog on the head and buckled in, and Petricia sat next to him and patted the empty seat between her and Char.

TH took it and Dokken jumped into his lap. "Is this how it's going to be?"

I swear the blood oath! Dokken exclaimed.

"Have you been watching those old movies with Kaeden again?"

You should try them, big human. They are most entertaining, and more importantly, relaxing, which is something you could use. You seem a bit uptight.

"I have a two-hundred-pound dog on my lap. It could be that."

Char petted Dokken's head as Terry scratched behind his ears. Petricia stroked the long hair on the dog's back.

The mechs climbed aboard, but faced the rear ramp. They were going to execute a combat drop in case the Benitons' sensor systems could determine if the shuttle landed. They would drop the team after flaring to slow the approach, then the drop ship would continue to the city.

That was Terry's plan. Once Kae and the team hit the ground, they'd be on their own with a second drop ship in orbit, ready for an emergency pickup.

The negotiation team was on their own too.

CHAPTER SIXTEEN

Nathan stood in the cargo bay of Federation Base Station Eleven. It wasn't his favorite space station since it was off the beaten path, but it had enough charm to keep him interested. He was on a short hop to recruit a group of traders for an intelligence mission. The cargo bay was filled with a variety of materials that could be transported innocuously to give the traders a cover story under any circumstance.

And to keep the Bad Company's trade arm robust and producing income.

They could also supply the covert intelligence section with information from across the Federation. The traders could ply the routes of systems contemplating joining to help Nathan better understand how best to leverage them.

That assumed General Reynolds wanted to bring them on board. Sometimes systems needed to mature before entering the fold, and sometimes systems were too self-serving to come on board. The general had no intention of making wealthy rulers even richer while their people suffered in poverty.

A scruffy-looking cargo ship finished its landing sequence.

Nathan leaned against a railing and watched as two men—one human and one Yollin—exited the hulking cargo hauler, the *ICS Fortitude*, and headed his way.

"Eight hundred and forty-two computer servers ordered by..." Jack glanced at the name on the shipping docket attached to his clipboard before he passed it over, "a Marcus Cambridge."

"Thanks," Nathan said, signing for the consignment before returning the clipboard and holding out his hand. Both Jack and Tc'aarlat shook it. "I'll get the dock crew to unload them. While they're doing that, can I treat you gents to a drink?"

"Sure," Jack said with a smile. "I never say no to a cold one."

"Sounds good to me," added Tc'aarlat, his mandibles tapping together. "Don't look a gift whore in the mouth, huh?!"

"'Horse!'" Jack corrected quickly. "Don't look a gift 'horse' in the mouth." He turned to Nathan. "Tc'aarlat's working on including human proverbs and phrases in his day-to-day conversation."

"He's, er...doing well," said Nathan, looking past the newcomers. "So, is it just the two of you?"

Mist ruffled her feathers and shrieked from her perch on Tc'aarlat's shoulder.

"Sorry," Nathan corrected. "The three of you?"

The Yollin reached up to scratch the top of the hawk's

beak, causing her to caw softly. "She doesn't like to be left out." He grinned.

"Tell me about it," Jack muttered under his breath.

Tc'aarlat shot him a brief look of irritation, but decided against bringing up Jack's intense dislike of his pet in front of their client. "There is another member of our crew here somewhere," he said. "Where's Dollen?"

Jack shrugged. "He disappeared as we finished docking. Said he wanted to get changed, since he had blood on his shirt." He noticed Nathan's raised eyebrows and added, "We had a little trouble on our way here..."

"Sorry!" called a voice from behind the group. Dollen jogged over to join them, sporting a jacket with the haulage company's logo branded on the breast pocket fastened all the way up to his throat. "Couldn't decide what to wear."

Nathan shook the Baloreon's hand, then led the small party through the customs and security zones to a large and well-appointed shopping mall filled with tourists of several species.

Sometimes it's nice to get back to the front lines and engage at the pointy end of the spear, Nathan thought. *And cut the head off a snake while recruiting a few new hands. I hope Ecaterina stays on the upper levels of the station, just until...*

"Drop in five!" Terry yelled. He flashed five fingers and held them up. Each of the four suited warriors held five fingers over their shoulders. Wearing the suits, they didn't need to turn around to see Terry. Their rear camera displayed what was behind them on their HUD. The colonel smiled.

He couldn't wait until he got his own.

"Not yet, lover," Char told him.

"I know. We're last." He turned to Char and they held hands as Terry angled his body so he could see the countdown timer as well as the team braced in the back of the shuttle Pod.

"*ONE MINUTE!*" Terry started bobbing as if psyching himself up to jump, and Dokken started barking.

"*MECH RECON!*" Kaeden yelled, boosting his speakers so the sound reverberated within the passenger compartment.

"*FLARING!*" Terry bent his knees at the same time as the mechs. The drop ship's nose pointed skyward as the gravitic drives pulled off most of the momentum, then the nose dipped and Smedley dropped the ramp.

"*GET SOME!*" Kaeden ran to the back and dove out, and less than a second later, the others followed him. The ramp closed and the drop ship accelerated toward the largest city.

Terry stopped rocking and breathed heavily. He stared at the closed ramp for a long time before he sat back down.

Kaeden turned around so the rockets on his lower legs could slow the suit before impact, then looked up and saw the others catching up. He hit the jets, and the others sped past. They slowed while maneuvering so they'd land in a diamond formation, everyone facing a different direction in case they came down with hostiles in range.

Marcie gave the all-clear sign, soon followed by Shonna and Merrit. They could sense no creatures in the landing zone, the "LZ."

The four mechs hit almost simultaneously at a speed that would have killed an unarmored human, and the dust of the dead zone clouded outward and upward.

The four had no need to wait for the air to clear before moving. Using a combination of infrared and other sensors to project the way ahead, Marcie took off at a run, boosting her stride as she accelerated on a beeline toward the inter-dimensional tear.

As she looked into the gray mists of the Etheric a beacon pulsed. It could be nothing else, and the power from it promised to be overwhelming.

"There's more juice flowing from that thing than we imagined," Marcie said over the suit's comm system as she ran.

"What does that mean?" Kae asked.

"It means that we could be supercharged to the point of overloading. In that case, we'll need your help."

Shonna and Merrit increased their spacing to the sides. Kae slowed until the diamond occupied more than a square kilometer.

"Three minutes to contact. Slowing approach. Do you see the external temperature?"

"One hundred and forty degrees. That'll put hair on your chest," Merrit offered.

"Suits for the win." Shonna started angling away from the group. "Contact at ten o'clock."

"I don't see anything," Kaeden replied.

"It's not on the HUD. I think we have a creature."

"I see it now," Marcie replied.

"You two check it out. Merrit and I will continue to the tear."

Marcie veered to the side and sprinted to Shonna's flank, leaving enough space to keep both from falling into a trap.

Kae sped ahead until he and Merrit were running in stride a hundred meters apart. Kaeden still couldn't see the tear, but Merrit signaled that they were getting close. Kae checked his HUD and saw that Marcie and Shonna had slowed to a walk.

"We're almost on top of it," Merrit reported, and stopped.

Kae took a couple more steps, then dropped to a knee. He frantically checked his sensors, but couldn't see anything.

"Look out!" Merrit cried before he opened fire.

Terry sat on the opposite side of the shuttle since Dokken didn't look like he was going to move. His tongue hung out of his dog face while Char and Petricia constantly petted him.

Jealous? Dokken asked.

Of course! Terry replied, using his comm chip. *Your plan is duct tape? We have got to get you a shipsuit.*

I figured that would help expedite the process.

I wish I had more control over it, buddy. We're in Nathan's service out here, so we don't always get to call the shots. We need armor, we need a custom shipsuit for my best buddy, and we need more people. If it's not one thing it's another, but for what it's worth I'm bumping your suit to number one priority if it's not ready by the time we get home.

Home? Dokken asked. *Do you mean the* War Axe *or Keeg Station?*

I think of Onyx Station as home. Weird, but good. At least I don't think of the ship as my wife like the captain does.

"Hey!" Mickey furrowed his brows and shook a fist at Terry.

"Hey, yourself! Can't a man have a private conversation with his dog?"

I'm not your dog.

"Don't make me come over there." Terry blew a kiss at the massive German Shepherd and Dokken leapt from his seat.

Terry twisted, but the dog still crashed down on him.

When the shuttle settled to the ground and the rear ramp opened Terry was corkscrewed, lying on the seat with Dokken straddling him and licking his exposed ear.

Joseph stood and bowed to someone that Terry Henry couldn't see, and Petricia and Char did the same. Micky was out of his seat and walking forward. Dokken delivered one last lick before jumping down. Terry freed himself and stood.

He wasn't prepared for what greeted him.

Kae couldn't see what Merrit was shooting at. "What's the target?" Kaeden maneuvered farther to the left.

"Can't you see it? One of those creatures is coming through the tear."

"I don't see anything!" Kaeden ran at a thirty-degree angle away from Merrit's railgun fire, and after a few steps it became clear.

They were behind the tear. Once past the portal, he could see the creature only too clearly. Three meters tall, with red leathery skin and horns. Merrit's rounds weren't penetrating the tear, and the creature was unharmed. Kae jumped back as the creature roared, but with railgun aimed he remembered his own orders.

Capture first. The creature bounded toward him and slashed with a mighty claw, but the long nails from a four-fingered hand scraped harmlessly across the armor. Kae rotated at the waist to guide the creature's momentum past his left arm.

Kae swung the railgun like a club, hitting the creature in the back as it passed. The power-assisted blow drove the creature face-first into the ground.

Kae tried to pin the beast, but it was up and spinning before he could get a good hold. Kae reared back to punch the creature with an armored fist as it swung its own clawed hand, and the claws faded for a millisecond *as they disappeared beneath the armor.*

The searing pain stopped Kae's blow. The claw had materialized inside the suit and raked through his chest. Kae jumped back quickly enough to limit how deep the claws dug, then raised his railgun and fired a stream of rounds. The creature faded as the first bunch passed through, but when it solidified the rounds ripped into it.

The creature howled and roared and Kae turned the external microphones down, but not off. The creature tried to return to a ghost-like state, but it could only maintain it for a second or two. Kae fired again, blasting the horned head apart, and the body fell to the ground and stilled.

Kae dropped to a knee, pain still coursing through him even though the nanocytes were attacking the injury with reckless abandon.

"Holy fuck, Merrit. Let's blast this portal to hell and go home." Kae grunted as he stood. "Merrit?"

Kaeden had taken one step when horns and a red head forced their way through the tear. Kae leveled his railgun and let it rip, and he kept up the fire until the creature went back where it came from. Kae limped a couple steps before realizing the pain was already gone, and hurried around the tear to find Merrit doubled over.

"Merrit?" Merrit was unconscious, and Kae had no idea why. He picked the werewolf up, tossed him over his shoulder, and started to run toward where he'd last seen Marcie and Shonna.

After half a kilometer he stopped to put Merrit down and called up his rockets, which popped up from behind his shoulder. He targeted them and sent four screaming downrange. They hit the target with a massive explosion, sending a red dust cloud skyward.

Although Kae couldn't see the Etheric energy, he could see the void where the dust cloud wasn't. The rockets didn't do any damage to the tear.

"That would have been too easy," Kae grumbled as he lifted Merrit to his feet. The man blinked his yellow eyes. "Are you okay?"

"Feel woozy, but that'll fade the farther I get from that thing."

"The creature?"

"The tear."

Kae nodded. "Let's go see how our better halves are faring. They have to be doing better than us."

CHAPTER SEVENTEEN

Terry put his hands on his hips and rolled his head. Behind the shuttle was nothing. There was no Beniton delegation. There were no buildings.

The others started laughing.

"Are your missions always like this?" Micky asked, having joined the spoof at the last second.

"Pretty much. You know what they say...paybacks are a mother." Terry forced a scowl at the group, but couldn't maintain it. He appreciated the quality of the practical joke.

"At least you don't have a stealth cat befouling your pillow every day," Micky lamented.

"You know Smedley is in on that," Terry said matter-of-factly.

Micky stopped and grabbed the colonel's arm, looking at him in disbelief.

"I asked him directly and he said 'no'!"

"He's evolved, which means he can lie."

"Our EI is lying to us? I mean, our AI..." Micky scratched his chin. "That makes the most sense."

"Are you coming?" Char asked from outside the drop ship.

When Terry and Micky exited, they found that Smedley had landed the shuttle on the edge of the city with the stern facing away. When they stepped into the open, they found that they were not alone.

"The Grays," Terry said softly when he saw the greeting party.

Joseph held his head as his face worked through a series of emotions. With a final wince he let go of it and bowed, and the others followed suit.

"My name is Captain Micky San Marino, and I am pleased that you decided to meet us." The captain walked forward but stopped more than an arm's length from the nearest of the gray-skinned, almond-eyed aliens. They looked dainty with their thin arms and bodies, and like the Crenellians they had oversized heads.

You gave us no choice once you defiled our space station, one of them said. Micky looked from one to the next, unsure which of the five present had spoken.

"Aliens are coming through the tear in the Etheric dimension. We're here to help stop them," Micky said pleasantly.

Who said we need help, let alone your *help?* the disembodied voice asked.

"Because it's not getting any better. They continue to come through the tear."

Micky looked back to Terry.

"We had a request to come here and deal with the interdimensional tear and the hell-spawn coming through to your planet," Terry explained.

You didn't get that request from us. It was probably one of the others. The Rift has brought us the Skrima, but we can shield our city from an Etheric intrusion. The shields isolate the Skrima near the equator. It is inhospitable to the point that they will eventually leave.

"You don't believe that," Joseph interjected as he touched his nose. Petricia held onto Joseph's arm.

A telepath. The oldest of you is the most evolved, it seems.

"Thank you." Joseph approached one of the Grays standing to the side. "I suspect you know what we really want, which is access to the miniaturized power supply technology. We suspect it caused the Rift in the first place. And if you aren't going to use your space station, we'd love to put a garrison aboard to help us expand into this section of space. We can limit who comes and goes so you are left in peace. If we don't people will show up unannounced more often than you'll like, including the Skrima."

Micky stepped back, shaking his head.

"It was worth a shot, Micky," Terry whispered as he stepped to the front. Char moved forward and stood by his side.

Four faced five, and none spoke.

"Okay," the Gray in front of Joseph said aloud.

"Okay what?" TH asked.

The information has already been transferred to your AI, now leave us in peace as you agreed. We will make things very uncomfortable for you should you violate the agreement.

"I believe you," TH said. He waved, and with a quick nod turned and headed toward the back of the shuttle. Dokken barked and ran after his human.

After the rest had climbed in, the rear deck started to close.

"Did they send you anything, Smedley?" Terry asked.

"Yes, Colonel Walton. In a single burst transmission they gave us the power source design and the access codes for the space station, along with instructions for how to repair the damage you caused."

"Damage that *we* caused because they weren't very congenial! We were protecting ourselves, but we'll fix it and then we'll occupy it." Terry licked his lips and grinned. "Here's to a quick negotiation!" Terry tapped his forehead with two fingers. "Smedley, can you link us to Kaeden for an update, please?"

"Hang on!" came the frenzied reply, but Kae left the channel open. The railgun fire in the background was unmistakable.

"Get us there, Smedley. Fastest possible speed," Terry ordered calmly.

He opened the forward locker as the drop ship lifted off and accelerated. As usual they weren't thrown backwards, because the gravitic drive prevented the transfer of gee forces to the inside of the ship.

Terry pulled out his Jean Dukes Special and strapped it to his hip, and handed Char her pistols and a railgun. Joseph and Petricia both took railguns, although Petricia looked at hers with a certain amount of disgust.

Micky held his hands up.

"Stay with the shuttle. There's a railgun in here for you just in case they get past us."

"Then Smedley and I will take off and go for reinforcements."

"They'll probably already be on their way. Here," Terry said as he handed ballistic vests and helmets to everyone.

"Hey, Dad," Kaeden said into the silence. "These things are real bastards to kill."

"Are you okay?" Terry asked. The others listened intently as they watched Char strap a flak jacket on Dokken.

"I am now. These creatures ghost in and out. Even after coming through to our dimension they can disappear back into the Etheric, but only for a few moments. And they can use that ability to penetrate our armor—one went claws-deep into my rib cage. But they splatter just like any meat bag when they reappear."

"We're on our way in. Are you ready for extract?"

"Sounds good. Home on our beacon. We dropped a few rockets on the tear, but that didn't do anything except kick up some dust. Three demons down, but I have no idea how many are on the planet. They are problematic to locate. We'll debrief when we're back on the ship."

"Understood." Terry picked at his fingernails as he leaned forward in his seat with his head bowed.

Char put her hand on the back of his neck. She had also felt that sudden pang at hearing that Kaeden had been injured. Even though they'd been at it for a long time, parents would always worry about their kids.

"ETA, Smedley?" Terry asked.

"Descending toward their beacon now. I'll drop the ramp in three minutes." Smedley waited before adding, "Ted is quite pleased with the information you acquired. He told me to thank you."

"He did not say that," Terry countered. "Since we have

you on the hook, tell the captain how you've been helping Wenceslaus."

"I don't believe I will. Prepare to recover the mech recon team." A buzz sounded over the speakers.

"That's all I need to know." Micky gave the hairy eyeball to the speakers in the ceiling. "How to pay you back...that's the question."

The drop ship hit the ground harder than normal, then the rear deck descended and four mechs walked aboard.

"We fired a shitload of ammo to kill three of them. We may have to rethink our strategy."

Ted looked over the information Smedley had forwarded on behalf of the Benitons. "Not only can we start building these right away, we can start integrating them into our systems because we have the energy parameters. It's been a good day, Ankh."

Ankh shivered with excitement, then they raised their holo screens and went to work.

"First order of business is building an Etheric power supply assembly line. Break down the components, Plato, and see how we can line them up..."

Ted and Ankh disappeared into their technology, as happy as two men could be.

Kimber was relentless. They started training the second

the drop ship left for the surface, and they were still training when the ship returned six hours later.

From weights to running to hand-to-hand, they rolled from one session to the next without taking a break.

"Ma'am," Sergeant Fitzroy panted. "Is there any way... the boys can call it a day? If we have to...go into combat tomorrow...we might be a little dogged."

"Boys?"

"I'm having...a hard time speaking...being out of breath and all...so 'boys' was much easier...than men and women. I apologize...for being overly pithy." Fitzroy took deep breaths between every few words. His short hair was matted to his head, and sweat streamed down his face.

Kimber was sweating, but not much. She'd trained harder than anyone else her whole life. Well, anyone except Marcie. They both had nothing to prove and yet everything to prove.

TH never let gender dictate any of his decisions. He put the best person into the position that needed to be filled or the job that had to be done. Nanocytes had been the great equalizer, giving people with a smaller stature like Kim and Kae the advantage of oversized strength without being genetically gifted with size.

Like Gene the werebear. He had been a man-mountain.

Kim turned away as she thought of her old friend and mentor. How was he holding up? What about the others?

"Training's done for the day! Hit the showers, and be ready for a mission brief at a moment's notice. We don't know when we'll go planetside, but it'll be soon." Kim hurried toward Ted's lab. She wanted to find out when the

IICS was going to be ready. She had a pain in her heart that needed to be filled by friendly voices from the next galaxy.

She started to run, as if not finding out would crush her. Her chest tightened and her legs became heavier with each step.

Kim passed Kaeden, Marcie, and her parents on the way, but she barely spared them a glance. They followed her as she ran through the corridors with the ease of familiarity.

She didn't hesitate upon reaching Ted's lab, despite a three-dimensional image telling visitors to go away. She used her code to override the door and walked in.

The others followed her and stopped as she planted herself inside the door. In front of her were swirling images from wall to wall and Ankh and Ted walked between them, touching various points in mid-air while motioning with their hands to fill gaps that only they could see.

Kim's mouth was open, but she hesitated to speak. Her overwhelming desire for an answer was balanced by her understanding that interrupting Ted could lead to the instantaneous delivery of an answer she didn't want to hear, whether it was true or not.

Ted crossed his arms and studied the swirling colors, and the Crenellian stopped what he was doing and stood still. Ted walked back and forth, touching one wall and strolling to the other, then clapped once and the holographic images disappeared. Ted blinked when he noticed he had visitors.

"Don't you people read signs?" he asked with a dismissive wave.

"Of course, but you know that we'll ignore them. Case in point." Char pointed to the open hatch and the group standing within.

Ted shook his head but Ankh showed no emotion, just watched dispassionately.

"When can I talk with Uncle Gene or anyone else we left behind?" Kim asked, having found her voice.

Ted pointed at one side of the room and then the other. "We just finished. All we need to do is manufacture the units and send them to Earth."

"Don't you need to test them?" Terry interjected.

"What do you think we were doing?"

"A simulation?" Terry looked with raised eyebrows at the werewolf genius.

"Yes, yes, but the simulation is one-hundred-percent accurate. They'll work. Smedley already has the design and construction criteria. We will be able to manufacture at least five complete units on the ship, but to fabricate any more we'll need additional raw materials—most of which we can acquire from the planet below."

"No can do, Ted," Terry said, holding up his hand. "We have an agreement with the Benitons, and mining their planet wasn't in there. The penalty for violating the contract is pretty stiff, so we'll find a different source for the raw materials. And if I'm not mistaken, we agreed to repair the space station and that will take four of the power supplies."

Char nodded.

Kim exhaled and looked at the deck, and Kaeden wrapped a protective arm around his sister's shoulder. "It's okay, Kim. We'll get them to Earth and to the people we care about even if we have to take them ourselves."

Terry gave Kae a thumbs-up. He and Char agreed with the sentiment.

"I'll tell Felicity that you'll take care of it." Ted started futzing with the box that contained Plato.

"Hang on," Kae began, but Kim grabbed his arm. "We'll take care of it."

Marcie nodded. Ankh remained stoic.

"Aren't you mortar forkers hungry?" Terry asked.

Char rolled her eyes.

"Yes, dear. We recognize that you're trying not to swear, but you're doing poorly at it. I'll have to ask Ramses, but I don't think that counts to give anyone a payout." Marcie shook her head. "Nope. You didn't swear today, so that makes Nathan a loser."

"I'm okay with that." Terry kissed Char on the cheek. "Good job, Ted. I'm sure the IICS will be a magical piece of hardware. We have debriefs, missions to plan, and chow to eat, not necessarily in that order, so we can walk with you to see Jenelope or we can carry you—those are your two choices. Come on, Ankh, time to go."

Ankh took one step before bowing to Ted. "All hail Ted."

"All hail Ted," echoed from the speakers.

"Would you stop that?" Char said, and pointed a finger as if correcting a child. Ankh mouthed the words in open defiance as Char loomed over him.

Terry laughed as he walked out. *Hail Ted? That'll be the day.*

CHAPTER EIGHTEEN

Timmons looked at a screenful of specifications.

A million metric tons of steel hung stationary in space, anchored by a gravity device that kept the random bits from floating away.

All Keeg Station needed was rhyme, reason, and a driven workforce to turn the raw material into a space dock.

"I don't see why it won't work." Timmons continued to study the numbers.

"It will if we can keep them going in the same direction," Sue replied, watching her mate and not his project plan. They'd co-managed hundreds of projects that brought San Francisco back to life as a thriving center of commerce in the world after the fall, so she didn't need to see his plan to know that it was sound. The only unknown was the workforce.

"Have they changed? Will they work for us without causing any problems? Last thing we need to do is entrust a starship to them and have them sabotage it—not because they're terrorists, but because—heaven forbid—they saw a *woman!*"

Sue gently pulled on his chin so he'd look at her and not the screen. "Once they start on this and see the possibilities freedom gives them, I think they'll blend into society rather quickly."

"The love of women is the root of all evil," Timmons intoned.

"I think that's the love of *money*, dear."

"I heard a homeless guy on the boardwalk in Atlantic City say my version. I think he was onto something."

Sue straddled Timmons' lap, but the chair protested the additional weight. He leaned back as her lips sought his, then flailed as the chair gave way and they tumbled to the floor.

They weren't bothered by the change of position, but their ears perked up when the hatch opened and someone walked in. They could see stylish shoes and shapely legs.

Felicity peered down at them. "Don't we have a ship-yard to build?" she drawled, shaking a finger in their direction. "Werewolves and their libidos, God love 'em."

Timmons winked at Sue and they climbed to their feet. "We have a plan," he said, grinning.

The *War Axe* in Orbit over Benitus Seven

"What the hell? You bring your stinkfest to the chow hall?"

Terry heard the voices from down the corridor. With idle curiosity, he looked for the speaker when the hatch opened and revealed that most of Bad Company's Direct Action Branch was already there and eating.

It wasn't difficult to pick out the offended and the offender. One man had his arm raised and was using his hand to wave air from his armpit toward a second man, who was shaking a fist. One second later, the offended launched himself over the table. He sent trays flying as he landed, and the two fighters rolled to the deck.

"STOP!" Terry snarled, and forced his way between the tables. He grabbed the man on top with both hands and picked him up, then kept lifting and turned as he bodily threw the warrior toward the hatch. The second man was wedged under the table, but Terry made quick work of him too. They both scrambled out the hatch, nodding to Kim and Kae as they bolted.

Terry looked angrily at Kimber, but softened at the look on her face.

Morale was fraying, hers included. That was why she'd gone to see Ted. All eyes were on Terry Henry as he turned back and surveyed the warriors and crew.

"Well?" Ted demanded from the corridor. "Are we going to eat or not? I have work to do."

Terry held his hands up, although the mess deck was already silent. "Ted is going to bring the space station to life, then we're going there on a liberty call! You might think that space station tried to kill us—and you'd be right —but it didn't win, because we're the Bad Company. We don't take that kind of crap. This place will blow your mind with its three-hundred-and-sixty-degree holographic projections. It's like nothing you've ever seen. I'll even send my personal stock of beer with you. Treat it well!

"While you're there, we'll be planning how to kick some demon ass. We'll recover from the party, and then go planetside. We'll hunt those bastards down and send them back to the hell from which they came. While we're out here, we're going to see what Ten has in store for us at Home World.

"And then we'll go home—to our new home, Keeg Station—where we'll take some time off. We'll take anyone who wants to travel the universe as a civilian to Onyx Station, where you can jump a transport and go on a real vacation. If you get arrested, you're on your own. If you don't, you're not trying hard enough!"

Get Ted and Ankh some damn chow and get him to work fixing the space station. I want that done today, Terry ordered over his comm chip. Marcie invited Ted and the Crenellian past the group and ushered them to the front of the line.

"Libo! Libo! Libo!" Fitzroy started to chant and forty other voices joined him, including Terry and the pack. The colonel walked between the tables, high-fiving the warriors as he continued the chant. When he reached Fitzroy they grasped hands and shook, slapping each other on the shoulder.

"What's for lunch? I'm starving," Terry declared. The chant turned into a cheer when Kaeden brought one of his old movies up on the screen—*Patton*. The crowd quieted as George C. Scott delivered his speech.

Jenelope waved and Terry worked his way to the kitchen.

"Yoga," she said.

TH looked down his nose at the ship's therapist and didn't answer.

"You heard me." Jenelope tapped a wooden spoon against her palm.

"Sunsets and palm trees," Terry replied.

"Get them into yoga."

"We're not doing yoga."

"Yoga."

"No."

Jenelope shook her spoon in TH's face.

"Maybe. But why?"

"Your people are on edge—it's been one death-defying act after another. You don't think your exploits on the station were shared with everyone? What about the planet? Did you hear how much blood was inside Kaeden's suit?"

Terry shook his head.

"Yoga."

"Fine." Neither Terry nor Jenelope moved.

"You'll start with a session this afternoon, then?"

Terry didn't answer, and Cory appeared behind him. "I would love to lead a session this afternoon. Put it on the schedule, Dad. Thanks, J! You're the best."

"You heard her. Put it on the schedule." Jenelope returned to tapping her spoon.

"Where did you find wood for your spoon?"

Jenelope raised one eyebrow. *Tap. Tap. Tap.* The spoon continued its rhythm.

Terry leaned over his shoulder and yelled, *"FITZROY!"*

"Aren't you supposed to be somewhere else?" Micky asked.

"We have a mission to plan," Terry replied as he continued to drill into the imagery of the terrain around the Rift.

Terry, Marcie, Kaeden, Christina, Merrit, and Dokken were the only others present in the captain's briefing room.

"Not into yoga?" Micky asked. The rest of the Bad Company were in the recreation room on their yoga mats.

Terry closed his eyes and turned toward the captain. "Everything has its time and place. Right now, the best thing I can do with my time is plan this next operation. Based on what Kae and Merrit saw at the Rift, these things are coming through with great frequency. There could be hundreds of thousands of them already on Benitus Seven. How in the holy hell are we going to send them back? Can we kill that many? Can we line them up and shove them through? How are we going to resolve this?"

Micky looked down at his lap. Despite the success of the negotiations with the Benitons Terry had returned carrying the burden of an injured son and an insurmountable task, and it weighed on him. For Terry Henry Walton, yoga wasn't the answer.

The captain wasn't sure what the answer was, though.

"My apologies, TH, for my ill-advised attempt at humor. I can't fathom the task before you, but if there is anything the *War Axe* can do, build it into the plan and we'll support you."

"I can't ask for better than that." Terry sniffed. He smelled something, but he couldn't figure out what it was. Dokken was lying on the deck at his feet, softly snoring.

"Kae, what do you think about engaging them directly? Is that a fight we can win?"

"No fucking way," Kae answered, rubbing his ribs where the Skrima's claws had penetrated. His subconscious rose to the surface, and he shivered as he remembered how close it had been. He had trusted his armor to protect him. The Bad Company wasn't going to beat up little kids on the playground. The enemy had teeth and a way to use them.

TH had expected an abrupt answer. "Merrit?"

"The Etheric. They are obvious and vulnerable there, but so are we."

"Explain more about how they are vulnerable? We only need to convince them that staying in this dimension is hazardous to their health. Getting them to leave of their own accord would be optimal, it sounds like," Terry replied.

Marcie looked like she wanted to talk, so Merrit offered her the floor.

"Working within the Etheric isn't something we can do. Our biggest link is pulling power from the dimension into our own. The Benitons have mastered that technology, and I think we need their help to send the Skrima a message. Imagine if we were able to send an ear-piercing whistle through the Etheric straight into the brains of these creatures! Either they'd go on a murderous bender, or they find a way to make the ugly noise stop by going back through the Rift."

"Could they stay in our dimension as an escape from the sound or whatever we project?"

"Yes, but then they'd be easy to kill." Marcie leaned back.

"There are too many of them," Christina started. Terry leaned back as she took a breath to continue. "In your doctrine, the force multiplier was essential in overcoming a numerically superior enemy. Whether a bigger bomb or blowing a dam or using weapons of mass destruction, the military does what it has to in order to achieve its stated objective."

"Of course," Terry replied, but Christina wasn't finished.

"Lines of communication. Logistics centers. Command and Control. These are an enemy's innate vulnerabilities, yet with the Skrima we haven't seen any signs of these potential targets."

"You're starting to sound like me," Terry said.

"I'll take that as a compliment. Just because we don't see them doesn't mean they aren't there, though. If we assume these creatures aren't intelligent, we should be able to herd them using fear once they see that they can be easily killed. But if they *are* intelligent, we should be able to appeal to their higher reasoning. The logic of being killed once they realize their natural defenses are gone. In the latter case, we don't have to create fear in every creature anew, only the ones who can tell the others that they need to run."

Terry nodded and smiled at Christina.

"We need to have a conversation with the Benitons again," Terry stated as he stood and started to pace. A smile tugged at the corners of his mouth. "I see a plan coming together. Everyone get to yoga. I'm going to talk with the general."

"Smedley?" Micky asked.

"Ted." Terry shook his head, but a deal was a deal. He had to beg Ted to build the weapon, because Terry had no faith that the Benitons would do anything outside what they already agreed to.

"Why don't you come, too, TH?" Marcie asked softly.

He headed for the corridor and without looking back, he said, "Maybe some other time. There's stuff I need to do, and not doing it wouldn't be very relaxing." Dokken followed Terry down the corridor as the others watched them go.

"Heavy is the burden of command," Micky intoned before excusing himself to return to the bridge.

"It's our job to make it easier on him, but he seemed content when he left," Marcie suggested.

"I know that look. It means he has a plan, but he needs to confirm a few details. In the interim, I'm looking forward to corpse pose," Kae said.

Marcie took his hand and they tried to psyche themselves up for yoga. Christina trailed them, shaking her head.

Merrit stayed behind. He didn't want to go. Two hundred years old, and he felt guilty about skipping school? "Goddammit!" He pushed himself away from the table. "Smedley, tell Shonna I'm on my way."

"She's expecting you," Smedley replied instantly.

"Of course she is." Merrit jogged after Christina, Marcie, and Kaeden. "Dammit."

Smedley? Terry asked as he watched Ted and Ankh put one of the Etheric power supplies back together. It was the one they had taken apart to reverse-engineer, but no longer needed. It was one of the four they would reinstall in the space station, and with the codes provided by the Benitons bring the station back to life with its full and complex holographic interfaces.

Yes, Colonel Walton?

When can I interrupt them?

I wouldn't advise that. I don't think any time is a good time to interrupt Ted when he's working, Smedley cautioned.

When is he going to finish?

When he is done.

Smedley, I remember the good ol' days when you didn't give me a ration every time I ask a question.

I think these are the best of days right now.

Finally we agree on something! Terry crossed his arms and leaned against the wall, settling in to wait as long as it took. He put his mind to work on the deployment details, and how to manage a planet full of creatures with a shuttle's worth of warriors.

All he needed was a force multiplier. *All hail Ted.*

Sonofabitch! he thought. *Here I am, hat in hand. I wish Felicity was here. This would be so much easier.*

Ted and Ankh finished putting the power supply together and started to leave. When they saw Terry, Ted pointed at Ankh. "Carry those for him."

TH trembled for only a millisecond before smiling and relieving the Crenellian of his burden. He didn't bother to ask where they were going, since it would be obvious soon enough.

Ted hesitated. "Grab the toolkit, too. We'll make this in one trip!"

Ankh stepped aside to give Terry room, since the toolkit was a large case.

At least it had handles. He put the power supplies on top before bending at the waist to better balance himself. He gripped the handles and stood, but the box resisted. He pushed with his legs until the toolkit rose from the deck, and Terry grunted with the effort. "What the hell is in this?"

Ted shook his head in exasperation. "Tools." Ankh was first into the corridor, and held the hatch open as Ted walked through. Terry struggled to follow as he balanced the tool chest with the power supplies on top.

"Hurry up! We haven't got all day," Ted called back. Terry couldn't see him around the huge chest.

"Are we going to the hangar bay, Ankh?" Terry asked between grunts.

"Yes. We are on our way to the space station to make the repairs."

"I'm taking the elevator," Terry said as he turned and headed the other way. "Come on, Dokken. I know you're down there somewhere."

I am. Don't tread on me, human.

Terry started to laugh. He couldn't control himself, and had to lean against the bulkhead. His chest heaved with the effort to stay upright.

"When all else fails, revel in the absurdity."

CHAPTER NINETEEN

Smedley flew the shuttle, as he always did. The docking was smooth, and the access through the airlock uneventful. They followed the access tube to where they'd burned through the emergency bulkhead, and passed the power supplies across the threshold one by one.

Ted and Ankh walked away before Terry could work the tool chest through, and he watched them go without saying a word. They weren't going to be much help.

"And keep it upright. Those are sensitive instruments in there," Ted said over his shoulder. He carried three of the power supplies, and Ankh carried one. Terry almost felt sorry for the Crenellian...until he looked at the tool chest.

Then the only one he felt sorry for was himself. Terry finally took a good look at the chest. It was four separate units latched together, but the latches were recessed. He popped the releases and broke the unit down. In moments, he had it through the hole in the bulkhead. He reassembled it into two sections and then made two trips to the lowest deck of the station, where an impatient Ted and a stoic Ankh waited.

The first section of the tool chest Terry had brought wasn't the one they wanted, so Terry ran up the stairs and returned shortly with the second chest. Arguing with Ted was useless, so Terry didn't bother.

Once the second half of the chest arrived, Ted got to work without a word of thanks to Terry for carrying it. TH stayed out of the way and thought back to the thousands of times he'd asked Ted for something. He remembered saying thank you after each exchange. Char always expressed her appreciation. Ted couldn't be bothered.

I don't need you to thank me, but I do need you to make a weapon.

Terry waited while they did their thing. The first hour passed, then the second, and it was well into the third before Ted looked at the work and grudgingly deemed it satisfactory.

He opened the box that contained Plato, and the two started talking mind to mind. The lights flashed throughout the station as it came online. The stale air was quickly rejuvenated, and the emergency bulkheads retracted. Even with only the three of them on board, the entire station came to life.

"That's it. Time to go back to the ship," Ted declared.

"Ted. I have a request."

"No. I won't help you carry the tools. That's work for minions like yourself."

Terry ignored the jibe. "We need a weapon to use against the Skrima, to flush them out of their partial existence in the Etheric dimension and solely into ours."

"We already have one of those." Ted threw up his hands and started walking away. "Bring the tools."

Terry lifted half the chest. "What do you mean you already have one of those?" he asked over the top.

"It's like a jammer—neutralizes the field so that those sensitive to the Etheric won't be able to tell someone is there."

"That doesn't sound like what I'm looking for," Terry replied as he negotiated the stairs. Ankh wasn't climbing quickly, or Ted would have hurried ahead.

"It works actively, pulling people out of the Etheric as much as masking the access to energy." Ted turned and stood with his hands on his hips. "But you don't want a small field generator. You want something that will work across the whole planet."

"Bingo. And then we want to herd the exposed Skrima back through the gate. I'm not up for genocide."

Ted's eyes unfocused as he communed with his AI. When he returned to the present, he replied, "We have a plan. Bring the tools."

Once on the main deck, they left the stairwell and walked toward the corridor that would take them to the shuttle. Ted abruptly stopped, and his head swiveled back and forth as he tried to take it all in.

Terry put the tool chest down and settled for gawking.

The main area was filled with color and activity. Trees swayed in an invisible breeze., and Terry would swear he felt the air moving with the motion of the limbs. Everything looked so real that he thought he could touch the new world into which he'd been thrust.

His hand slid through a rocky outcropping, stopping

when his fingers reached the railing. The scene in the atrium was one of outdoor splendor—a jungle wonderland painted in vivid color.

Terry felt refreshed, as if he were actually in a wild forest. The effect was pronounced, even for Ted. Ankh looked shocked. Terry realized that the Crenellian had probably never been in a forest before.

TH picked the alien up and let him sit on his forearm, their heads close together as Terry pointed out the wonders of the flora and fauna. Birds and small furry creatures made their presence known, not just by sight but sound, too. Terry swore he could hear a rabbit-like creature in the underbrush, as well as the crunch of his boots on the grit and grass.

"I'll have the jammer in place within a day," Ted said conversationally as he strolled through the central area. He peeked into an office, where the desk was now filled with personal items and even a three-dimensional interface where someone could interact with the system.

All of it holographic projections that reacted to the beings within.

Terry put Ankh down, and he ran to Ted's side. The two held hands like a father and a son would as they discussed the computing power behind the system.

Of course that's what you see, Terry thought as he picked up the top half of the tool chest and hurried down the now-filled corridor toward the shuttle. The bulkhead had retracted, allowing TH through. He stepped around the piece they had cut out and almost ran into two full-sized bots. He thought they were projections until they bumped him aside. He let them pass.

They picked up the section of bulkhead and rose toward the ceiling. Hover technology wasn't new, but he suspected the bots were using something different than what the Federation was used to.

So much new technology that they'd been given, but now payment was due. The cost? Close the Rift and rid the planet of the Skrima.

"The ship is so much quieter without the platoon," Kimber said, and Auburn nodded slowly.

"I can't hear the difference," Terry said. Char nudged him with her elbow. Kaeden had a long face. "Out with it."

"There's a party, and we're stuck over here," Kae replied.

"Is that how you see it?" Terry asked.

Kaeden nodded, followed by the others. Cory and Ramses shrugged before adding their nods.

"Darn it," Terry said.

Ramses shook his head and pulled out his notepad.

"Go on, then. We're connected through the forward airlock. Go and join the party. We'll reconvene tomorrow morning for the final mission brief. We'll conduct team briefs in the hangar bay, and then perform a combat drop using all six shuttles. As usual, party now, because once we hit the planet we're not stopping until we've accomplished the mission."

"Understood," Terry's senior team replied—their family and Char's pack. TH watched them go, and Char watched him.

"As you said, 'out with it.'" She poked him in the side.

"I have a bad feeling about this one."

Char traced her hand up his arm and rubbed his shoulder. "It couldn't be worse than Poddern."

"I suppose not, but what if Ted's thing doesn't work? How can we close the Rift?"

"Ted's device will work, but what do we do with it? If there are a hundred thousand of those things running loose down there we're fucked. The difference is, we'll see how fucked we are."

"You're trying to bait me into swearing, because you know I agree with you. I'll add my two cents worth here, in the privacy of the conference room. Upside down and backwards. Triple-lindy screwed, and we'll still give it all we've got. I don't think we'll close the Rift, but we will have to monitor it continuously and kill anything that tries to come through."

"I think you're right, TH. Closing that doorway could release an untold amount of energy, and we can't risk that. The Benitons might be a little gruff, but they don't deserve to have their planet torn apart."

"The Grays. Eons before the fall we laughed at people who saw UFOs and claimed to have been taken, and here we are on a planet populated by Grays. They probably abused humans in all kinds of ways, yet we're standing between them and demons from hell—but that's what makes humanity great." Terry smiled at his wife, and her purple eyes sparkled back at him. "Exporting justice, because we will always be the good guys, as long as you don't get on our bad side."

Char stood and pulled Terry up with her. "Going to the party?"

"Nah. You know how it is when the commander shows up—puts a damper on the fun. I'll let them drink my beer in peace."

"You can get more beer, lover. By all that's holy! You and your beer."

"You knew about me and beer before we got together."

"You called that swill 'beer,' which should have told me to steer clear of you. We couldn't let Margie Rose think she wasn't a matchmaker, though. I did it for her."

"Long live Margie Rose!" Terry smiled. "Now I want a beer."

"So you *are* going to the party."

"No, I'm just going to get myself a beer. It's the least I can do before we drop."

"I'm talking about the party in our quarters." Char walked away.

Terry hesitated for a moment.

Better go after her, Smedley suggested.

You got that right, Terry replied.

Smedley saw everything that happened on the ship, and recorded most of it. He'd been waiting for the colonel to swear, but he didn't. Ramses would be disappointed, because the credits were starting to swing in Terry's favor.

Sheri's Pride

Timmons stood with his hands on his hips, wearing a spacesuit that he'd borrowed from Keeg Station. It wasn't quite the powered armored mech suits that the Bad

Company used. It had a minimal heads-up display, and it didn't have powered assist for the limbs. It was cumbersome in gravity, but it worked in space.

He still didn't like it. He looked at the army of faces wearing the extravehicular suits they'd recovered from Ten's fleet. He activated his suit's communication system and projected his words to every single member of the new workforce.

"Today is the day that we start building a shipyard—your shipyard. This is where you'll work, refurbish ships, and earn money you can use to do whatever you want. Live as free people live. At some point you may decide that you don't want to work in the shipyard anymore, and at that point the decision will be yours—but unfortunately not yet. You were the enemy a few weeks ago. Give us some time to get used to each other, become friends, and then you'll be free to choose. In the interim, we have a shipyard to build."

"Mister Timmons, sir?" a familiar voice replied.

"Yes, Brice, and it's just 'Timmons.'"

"I've been talking to the guys, and we want to name the shipyard 'Felicity's Hot Metal.'"

Timmons choked back the sound that rose involuntarily.

"I like it, gentlemen," Felicity drawled. "But if you must name it after me—what an incredible honor, by the way—but if you must, then may I suggest 'Spires Harbor, a waystation of hope and rejuvenation?'"

Does she still go by Spires? Timmons asked Sue.

She does. I wonder why she didn't take Ted's last name.

Timmons thought for a moment. *What is Ted's last name?*

I thought you knew, because I don't.

That's probably why she didn't take it. I can guarantee you that he hasn't told her, either.

"Felicity Spires, Governor of Spires Harbor," Brice said, and a number of voices murmured approval into their suit microphones. "And we know you don't have a name for us, but we'd like one. How about 'the Harborians?'"

"Done!" Timmons declared before he lost control. "Now it's time to start building Spires Harbor. If you'll bring up the schematics by slaving your pads to your HUDs as we showed you, you'll know your roles. We're going to shuffle out the hangar doors and get to work."

Dionysus had broken the project plan into individual tasks based on four-hour shifts for a five-hundred-man work party. When the first group returned, the second group would head into space and pick up where the first group left off.

Timmons was first through and into space, reveling in the lack of encumbrance in zero-gee. The bulky suit started to feel normal.

"Dionysus, when the workforce is clear, let's move the ship into position."

The mass of bodies drifted into space, unseen pneumatic jets maneuvering them into position. Many of the workers hung onto each other while one would use his attached thruster pack.

The group moved upward, grabbing the spine of the infrastructure already in place—a single metal beam hundreds of feet long with four transverse beams attached.

That was the entirety of the shipyard that had been put into place so far.

Keeg Station had not previously had the manpower or project managers for the work. With Sue and Timmons plus the Harborians and the AI Dionysus, the pieces were now in place.

Sheri's Pride shifted position. Thrusters engaged for attitude control and micro-maneuvering. It approached the framework and stopped.

"Put the attachments into place. Welders up!" Timmons called, even though the AI had already delineated the tasks and the workers saw them on their HUDs. Many were already moving when Timmons spoke.

He was obligated, just like Terry Henry was obligated to say "Wagons ho" whenever the group moved out.

It made no sense besides tradition. *The Harborians.* Timmons chuckled to himself. He didn't care what they called themselves. He hadn't encouraged a name—although he probably should have—but sometimes things worked themselves out.

The workers strapped beams together while bots performed the welding. Humanity was too frail in the older-style spacesuits to risk a torch burning through a suit.

One after another, the beams went into place. *Sheri's Pride* was becoming the hub of a vast shipyard.

Spiderlike legs would dangle beyond and below the ship and more legs would be added to hold ships steady as major or minor repairs were made. Directly below the *Pride* a full-service dock would eventually take shape, with gantries and a structure in which a ship could be put together from prefabricated components.

Timmons activated his jets and flew into space so he could take it all in.

"Dion, can you overlay a projection of the future shipyard over what I'm seeing?"

A scaled and textured image appeared on Timmons' HUD. *Sheri's Pride* disappeared within a great structure. The geometric balance of Spires Harbor was broken up by the projection of ships from the anchor points. In the projection the *War Axe* clung to one of the legs, and the vast ship looked small compared to the immensity of the Harbor. Timmons blinked the image away, leaving only what was before him.

"Much work to do, Dion, but the first weld has kicked it off. I wish I knew what TH and the others were up to." Timmons remained floating in space, serenely watching the bevy of Harborians work. Over five hundred suited men crawled over the outside of *Sheri's Pride*, and flashes of light signaled where the bots were finalizing the attachments.

Timmons breathed deeply and closed his eyes. Within his helmet, he heard music from Mozart's *Cosi fan Tutte*. He hadn't asked for it, but it seemed appropriate for that place and that moment in time.

CHAPTER TWENTY

The *War Axe*

Sixteen mechs were parked in the hangar bay as Colonel Terry Henry Walton stalked back and forth in front of the entirety of Bad Company's Direct Action Branch.

Even Ted and Ankh were there, although they weren't going planetside. The *War Axe* had made three high-speed passes in low orbit to deposit the satellites that contained the Etheric jammers. Ted and Ankh would control the signal from the ship and adjust on the fly to deliver exactly the right amount of counter-energy.

"Team leaders, have you issued the mission orders?" Terry asked.

"Sir, yes, sir!" came the bold replies.

"I expect that they'll run soon enough. Keep the way to the Rift clear, because that will mean fewer bodies to clean up."

Some of the warriors grinned, and others chuckled out loud. None of the senior leadership changed expression.

"When we activate the weapon we may be blinded too, but that evens the field—which means we have the advantage." Terry pulled his Damascus steel Mameluke sword from its scabbard and whistled it through a cross before him. In his other hand he held his Jean Dukes Special.

Christina hefted her boarding axe in one hand, and in the other was a railgun. One to the next, the weaponry and firepower carried by the small unit known as the Bad Company was overwhelming.

Was it enough to tame an entire planet?

"How do you eat an elephant?" Terry asked.

"One bite at a time," Marcie answered.

"Oorah," Terry replied softly. "One well-aimed round at a time. One enemy down, and then the next. Let's send these sons of wenches back to hell."

"Suit up!" Kaeden ordered and fifteen warriors left the formation to join him. Familiar faces and names—Praeter, Capples, Kelly, and more. They climbed in, buttoned up, and cycled the systems as part of a functions check.

Sixteen mechs with sixteen unarmored warriors as partners. They'd deploy two by two because they had to cover a lot of territory. Being bunched up might have been safer, but it would not have accomplished the mission.

That had been Terry's reasoning, and no one disagreed.

They split up, either two or three mechs per drop ship plus the warriors, the Weres, the vampires, and the enhanced.

Bundin ambled aboard with Dokken.

Extra water supplies had been loaded into the shuttles, and the ballistic canisters had been loaded with ammunition and water in case combat expenditures exceeded estimates.

Terry's estimates. He was counting on a few pieces of the puzzle to fall into place. By way of the shuttle's boosted communications system, he had a direct line to Ted. Timing would be critical for his plan to work.

The colonel surveyed the hangar bay. Once the drop ships had been loaded, it was as if they'd never been there. Terry twirled his finger in the air, and one by one the drop ships buttoned up. He strapped in as the ramp closed on his shuttle.

"Smedley, begin the countdown," Terry ordered.

"From three. Two. One." The drop ships launched into space simultaneously and then assumed unique vectors toward the atmosphere. Using the hot zone as a buttress, they planned to clear the northern hemisphere first, then exfiltrate and conduct a similar operation in the southern hemisphere.

Less than fifty people in teams of two.

The drop ships skipped and burned as they descended, but once into the clear air it was time.

"Ted, activate the weapon," Terry said, and Smedley made sure the signal got through. In moments Charumati started to blink and looked around her, tilting her head.

Cory's eyes stopped glowing and panic seized her. "I can't heal anyone!"

Terry flexed his arm. He felt weak and suddenly tired. He growled. "Power through it, people. The nanos are now drawing power from you! Eat some jerky or a protein bar. These creatures are going to be suffering, too, but I know *we* can operate without the Etheric energy. I am betting that they cannot. We're here for a reason, people, because in the whole universe there's one fighting force that can adapt, that can operate no matter what they're up against. The Skrima can stand by. Here comes the Bad Company."

He started to rock as he prepared for the landing.

"Ted, activate the infrared sensors and let's see what we see."

The front screens of the six shuttles were overwhelmed by heat signatures from the planet. Incrementally, Ted engaged filtering algorithms until the screen cleared up.

"How many Skrima are we looking at?" Terry asked, seeing few blips.

"Four hundred and twelve," Smedley replied.

"Thank God! Adjust drop locations to maximize engagement envelopes." Terry unbuckled and moved close to the screen. He blocked the view from the other passengers, but something had tickled his brain. "The Skrima are exclusively in the northern hemisphere, but they're not bunched up. It looks like they hunt in pairs."

"New drop locations are highlighted on the screen," Smedley reported.

Terry stepped aside for all to see. The mechs remained facing the rear deck, but Terry had no doubt their cameras were zoomed in on the screen—unless Smedley was projecting the images directly onto their HUDs.

"Kimber. I need you to take three teams and set up a blocking location here." Terry traced a location between the northernmost Skrima and the Benitons' largest city, and Smedley added it to the screens in all the drop ships. "Those overachievers need to have the errors of their ways explained to them."

"Yes, sir," Kim replied through the ship's speakers from her shuttle.

"Marcie. Take three teams and set up a line here, farthest west from the Rift, and start pushing them east."

"Kaeden. Same in the east. Don't let any of the Skrima get past you. Christina. You are the hammer. Take three teams and stay along the transition from the hot zone. If they try to head into Wasteland, finish them. If they are heading for the Rift, make sure they have a clear shot. Each team will be covering hundreds of miles. Call the drop ships if you have nothing in front of you and a long way to go. We'll leapfrog the teams as necessary."

Terry ticked off the players in his mind before continuing, "Joseph will be here with two teams. Aaron and Yanmei will be here with two teams. Cory, Ramses, and Auburn, you're in this gap due north of the Rift. I'll be at the tear with Char and Bundin. Dokken. It's too hot for you out there. I want you to go with Cory to protect her."

I understand, but I don't like it.

"I don't like it either, buddy, but it'll be a lot cooler where they are, which is where I'd prefer. I doubt I'll enjoy losing half my body weight in sweat."

The screen showed the drop ships heading in. The first two landed, disgorged a team, and raced skyward again. Like a frog hopping lily pads, the drop ships deposited their teams along a broad arc across the northern hemisphere, using terrain to delineate between areas of responsibility.

In some cases the warriors were a hundred kilometers apart, and in others only two. The warriors in mech suits saw exactly where the Skrima were, thanks to Ted's satellite system. The enemy didn't fade from view because they were blocked from using Etheric energy.

Unfortunately, so was everyone enhanced with nanocytes.

Kimber ran from the drop ship, the first to do so. "Lead from the front" was her father's motto and she embraced it, never shying from a fight. Kelly, decked out in her mech suit, ducked as she exited the shuttle, which lifted off without bothering to close the ramp.

"Targets?" Kim asked.

"Two this way, one kilometer." Kelly hatcheted her arm to show the way.

"Lock and load, and let's go say hi!" Kim took off running, but it was nothing like what she was used to. It felt like she was wading through molasses, so she got angry and let the adrenaline feed her. The nanos started to pull energy from her body to give that boost back and she picked up speed, but knew she wouldn't be able to maintain it.

Kelly loped along beside her. The suit helped offset some of the effects of Ted's Etheric-neutralizing weapon.

They ran through a field of wild grasses and sparse trees. The Skrima were in a copse at the far side. The two put a hundred meters between them. Kelly ran with her railgun raised, ready to fire. Kim's JDS was in her hand, swinging with her arms to help her maintain momentum.

"Your two other teams have landed and are on the move."

Kim didn't reply, since she needed her air. When Kelly slowed, so did Kimber. She brought her pistol up and weaved as she walked, looking over the sights and ready to fire the instant she spotted her target.

Soon enough the Skrima came into view, but they were wandering in circles with vacant expressions. Kim took aim, but couldn't fire. Kelly held her railgun steady, waiting on the order to unleash the weapon.

Kim pulled her comm device from her pocket and keyed it to broadcast to all personnel. "We've encountered the Skrima. They are confused, and not aggressive. I don't think they see us even though we're standing right here. Orders?"

Terry Henry's voice crackled through. "Get them to move, no matter what you need to do to accomplish that. We don't have the transport, so they'll need to haul themselves back to the Rift."

"Roger. Out." Kim stuffed the comm device back into her pocket. "Come on there, nice Skrima. I need you to get moving."

Kim held her pistol steady, having recovered her breath from the short run.

The creature finally seemed to notice her. It opened its mouth and made guttural noises. The second Skrima stopped meandering and stood shoulder to shoulder with his comrade.

"Not sure what's going on, but I don't like it," Kelly said using the suit's external speakers.

The Skrima hissed at her, and faster than the eye could follow they both charged. Kim snap-fired into one's face and blew its head off, but the other bowled her over. Her ballistic vest stopped most of the attack from the second creature, but her arm was unprotected. The claws raked across her forearm as they both tumbled to the ground.

Kelly danced around, trying to get a clear shot.

Kim tried to kick the creature away, but he was much larger than her and had better leverage. She caught his wrist as it slashed toward her head, but he grabbed her wrist and gripped tighter and tighter. Kim knew the bones would give way soon.

She screamed in fury and bucked as she tried to free herself, then the Skrima's head jerked sideways as Kelly butt-stroked it with her railgun. With its skull caved in, it collapsed. Kim kicked the dead Skrima off her. Blood trailed down her left arm.

Kim holstered her Jean Dukes Special and used her free hand to tie a bandage around the wound. She grimaced and held one end of the tie-off in her mouth, pulling tightly on the other. Blood leaked through.

"Ahh, for the good old days when we could shrug off injuries. I miss them." She tried to show bravado, but the injury scared her.

She activated her comm device. When Kelly picked her up to carry her to their next set of targets, Kim screamed in pain. "Son of a mother fuck, that hurt!"

"Report!" Terry replied.

"Don't believe them. The Skrima still have super speed, and once they realized we were there it was game on. They are faster and stronger than us. Do *not* let them close on your position. They ignored the mech and both came after me. And if you get a claw job, that shit hurts and the nanos aren't healing it." Kim tried to relax as Kelly loped across the uneven terrain.

"Two more targets six kilometers out."

"The others?" Kim asked.

"Four Skrima down. They are advancing." Kelly tried to maintain an even voice, but blood from Kim's wound ran down the front of her armor.

"Roger," Terry finally replied. "Hang on for another thirty minutes. We have something coming that will help you out."

Kae heard the report from his sister, and his lip quivered as a snarl formed. He had been the second-last on the ground, and felt like he was behind. The run hadn't bothered him as much as he thought it would, even though he was in a suit.

The railgun felt heavier than normal, but he had no intention of going into combat without it. His rockets had been reloaded, and he was ready to use them.

Kaeden picked two Skrima that were between his team and the next one. He targeted the rocket and sent it on its way. Other mechs were doing the same to increase the amount of space they could cover.

He tallied the other teams' reports and found that none of the Skrima had run. *Good,* he thought. *I like an enemy that is willing to stand and fight. It's stupid, but hey...we're giving them the choice.*

As he and his partner zeroed in on a pair of Skrima

ahead, they saw what Kim had seen. The demon-looking creatures wandered aimlessly, eyes unfocused.

"Sniper mode," he whispered from the suit's speakers, and his teammate moved to the side and covered his ears. Kae took aim and fired, then rapidly adjusted to the second target and fired a spread of three rounds in case the Skrima moved.

It didn't. Both Skrima exploded from the impact of the hypervelocity rounds. "Mark. Two down. Advancing," Kae reported. He checked his HUD to find his team efficiently moving forward.

"Maintain your spacing. Rockets to grid seven, Cap."

"Aye, aye, sir. Targeting. Firing." In his mind, Kae could see Capples' half-smile as he tracked the rockets through the sky. "A custom delivery by airmail," he would say—something that the blimps had brought back to a recovering Earth.

Airmail was the fastest way to deliver a package to friends and family.

"Your package has been delivered. How would you rate the service you received today?" Kae mumbled as the two IR targets disappeared after the rocket's impact.

CHAPTER TWENTY-ONE

Terry had landed his shuttle and kept it on the ground. He stood where he could see the screen, preferring to be outside despite the nearly unbearable heat.

The Rift was a kilometer away, but they were on the side where he could see it with his naked eye. "Smedley, set an alarm if anything comes through or if anything approaches."

"Of course, Colonel Walton. I'll notify you the second a creature comes through the Rift. None of the Skrima appear to be inclined to run from the Bad Company. There are none approaching."

Terry kicked at the dead ground, and wisps of dust rose into the air before slowly settling back in. There wasn't a breath of wind, and the air smelled like the dust of the Wastelands. No humidity. No life. Terry imagined that if Mars had air, it would smell the same way.

Bundin lounged outside the drop ship, his four eyes taking in the surroundings. "Finally, some decent weather," the Podder said conversationally.

Char remained inside. The shuttle's climate control system kept the inside cool by using the atmospheric shield that covered the rear opening. It shimmered occasionally as dust flitted off its surface.

Terry took a long drink of water. He listened carefully to the team reports Smedley funneled directly to his comm chip.

"How many Skrima down?"

"Over one hundred. This is going more quickly than I projected."

Terry looked at the monitor. "I think we're right on schedule. Why was your estimate different?"

"The unknowns. I calculated the number of Skrima and came up with a projection that was quite high. You seem to have ignored the extreme, correctly so, but how did *you* know? I had no data to suggest such a small number was possible."

"Gut feel, General. Moving a mass of soldiers onto a battlefield is a major logistical undertaking. I don't think they can feed here. It was my impression that they are creatures of the other dimension, and need to be there to survive. They are here to explore and wreak havoc, but not to live. A hundred thousand of them? They couldn't get through or back quickly enough to sustain such a number."

"I'll be," Smedley conceded.

"*Emergency.* Kimber is unconscious from loss of blood. Request emergency extract."

"Stand by," Terry replied. "Break. Break. Ted, turn off the jammer so Kimber can start her recovery. All units, hold your advance and dig in. Ted, give me fifteen minutes, then turn it back on, please."

The effect was instantaneous. Terry's chest seemed to swell with the power that the Etheric flooded into his nanos. Char walked through the shield and joined Terry in the heat. She kept her hands on her pistols. Bundin remained unaffected.

"Kelly?" Char asked.

"Alert!" Smedley blasted from the shuttle's speakers. "A creature is coming through the Rift."

Terry took aim and with his strength, he dialed his JDS to eleven. He braced himself and fired at the form moving within the tear.

The impact vaporized the Skrima, but the explosion on this side of the void was minimal. Terry clenched his teeth as he worked the pain from his shoulder. "Where was the Earth-shattering kaboom?" he asked in a high-pitched voice.

Char elbowed him in the ribs. She closed her eyes and explored the movement of power from the Etheric. When she opened them, she smiled. "I expect anyone who was on the other side of that opening is having a really bad day."

"Maybe we pop a round in there every now and then?" Terry offered.

"What if they pop back?" Char countered.

Terry squinted to see the Rift better. It had returned to its former state—a small swirl in the middle of nowhere.

"Then we probably don't want to be anywhere near there. We haven't seen any kind of technology from them, so I'm not sure they *can* shoot back."

"*Terminator?*"

"Where only organic material could travel through time? I don't buy it. I think they are intelligent, but not technologically so. I can't discern a purpose. There's no rhyme or reason to what they're doing besides murder and mayhem. What's their end game?"

"I don't know. Smedley?"

"I got nothing."

"I love the new you, Smedley," Terry replied.

"Kelly? Anything from Kimber?" Char asked.

"Kim here. Thanks for the boost. I'm slugging all our water now. Give me five minutes more and I'll be back in the saddle."

"That's good news," Char said, relief in her voice and on her face.

"Report!" Terry called.

"We're blind out here," Kae replied first. "Once the interruption in the energy flow was reinstated, the Skrima disappeared from IR. Stay frosty, people!"

"We've continued to advance. These creatures are ghosts in the mist, but we can still see them. We've got two teams converging on a pair now. They're moving, and we don't want them to get away. FIRE!" Christina yelled all of a sudden. The sound of railguns opening in automatic mode filled the channel, then there was a brief pause.

"Christina?"

Before she could answer the railguns opened up again, then just a mech's oversized gun continued to bark. "Dieee!" came a Pricolici voice.

Praeter had been assigned as Christina's suited companion. He hadn't worried about being able to keep up, and was mildly surprised that she was hard-pressed to keep up with him even in her reduced state.

When the power came back on, his HUDs blanked out. Christina smiled and used her power to see what was in front of them. She announced that the Skrima were coming so Praeter prepared himself, counting on her to point the enemy out before they got too close. He had heard Kimber's report, as they all had, and it put him on edge. If they were fast before, he expected them to be little more than blurs now.

He rotated his railgun through a figure eight before him, ready to fire the instant he saw anything.

Christina's comm chirped. Colonel Walton was calling for a report. She waited, and then started talking. In the middle of her report the Skrima appeared from the brush without disrupting any of the foliage, and like laser beams they headed straight for the pair of warriors.

Praeter didn't wait. He fired, spraying the hypervelocity darts back and forth between the inbound demons. They continued to run, unaffected by the railgun, although they started to dodge. Both Praeter and Christina stopped firing.

The Skrima solidified and the warriors fired again. One of the Skrima buckled as a volley hit it before it ghosted back into a semi-rigid state, but the creature shrugged off its injuries and started running again. Christina threw her railgun down and changed into her Pricolici form. Still holding her boarding axe, she charged.

Praeter slowed his fire, tracking the second Skrima until it was too close. The moment it raised its clawed arm to slash the mech, Praeter launched himself sideways while continuing to fire. The Skrima missed digging a claw into Praeter's chest and solidified for a fraction of a second, which was long enough for a railgun round fired from point-blank range to explode its head.

The mech turned, but Christina and the Skrima were tied up in hand-to-hand combat. She twirled her axe before her to hold its claws at bay, but it didn't care about the axe. It stabbed a claw forward like a single dagger, and it plunged into Christina's chest. She raked her own claw down the creature's arm and it screamed in pain.

Praeter tried to get a clear shot in the moment that the Skrima was vulnerable, but when it pulled back it ghosted out. Praeter fired anyway, but the darts passed straight through it.

Christina staggered backward, happy to have the nanos hard at work repairing what would otherwise have been a fatal wound. She charged a moment later, estimating when the creature would solidify to deliver its deadly counterattack. She dove to the ground and swung her axe, and was rewarded with a satisfying crunch.

While she was out of the line of fire, Praeter pounded the creature with hypervelocity darts. Once solid, the Skrima was finished. Huge chunks of flesh were blown off in a final frenzy of death.

Christina rolled away, but it was too late. She was already splattered in gore.

She started to change back into human form when the jammer came back on. She didn't have enough energy to complete the transformation, but her Pricolici form drew everything she had left. She passed out and fell over.

Praeter was too far away to catch her.

When the energy from the Etheric returned Cory's eyes started to glow blue again.

"You're back!" Ramses declared as they surveyed the open field. They hadn't moved since their arrival, waiting on word that the way ahead was clear. Without a mech or the ability to see into the Etheric, Cory considered their role to be almost useless.

"We need to get on a drop ship and be ready to respond in case something happens," Cory stated.

"We're supposed to hold position here to make sure nothing comes through this gap in our lines," Ramses replied matter-of-factly.

Dokken's eyes rolled back in his head as the German Shepherd shifted onto his back in his attempt to find a comfortable position to sleep.

Cory looked at the railgun in her hand, then back at the horizon. She shook her head.

Relax. It's a dog's life here, Dokken told them.

"That's what I'm afraid of." Ramses leaned his ear toward the pouch on his chest where the comm device rested. "Sounds like the Skrima are on the move. I wish we could see something."

Cory shielded her eyes from the sun as she scanned the horizon. Dokken barked and scrambled to his feet. When Ramses turned, the Skrima were on them. He used his railgun to block a slash. He tried to back away, but it attacked relentlessly. Ramses was forced to defend himself, unable to bring the dangerous end of the railgun to bear.

The Skrima howled as a massive German Shepherd

buried his teeth in the back of its leg, and Ramses dropped the butt of the railgun and fired from the hip. Three hyper-velocity darts tore through the creature's chest.

Cory was firing at a creature ghosting back and forth before her. Each time she let off the trigger, the Skrima darted in. Ramses added his firepower to hers to keep the Skrima from solidifying.

Cory backed away, but the demon remained close so Ramses maneuvered to keep his line of fire open. The Skrima dodged, and Cory's weapon stopped firing. She looked down in panic to see one of the Skrima's claws embedded in the firing mechanism. She could feel its hot breath on her face, and she closed her eyes.

"NO!" Ramses yelled, and jumped to her side just in time to catch the full sweep of the Skrima's long claws.

Ramses grunted and pulled the trigger and the railgun barked, sending a stream of projectiles through the creature which cut it in half.

The railgun continued to fire long after the Skrima had fallen and Cory grabbed her husband as he started to drop, his finger frozen on the trigger. She kicked at the railgun and it fell away as they went to the ground. She rolled on top of him and pressed her hands to the gaping wounds that had shredded his chest, ripping his heart apart.

Her hands glowed blue as the nanocytes raced from her into the torn flesh and she breathed heavily to hasten the surge, but the glow stopped the instant the jammer flooded the planet with its Etheric-countering field.

Ramses was dead, and she was powerless to bring him back. She fumbled for her comm device. "Turn it on! Turn it back on!" she cried.

"The Skrima are overrunning our people," Terry replied.

"Ramses is dead, and he'll stay dead if you don't turn the fucking power back on!"

"Ted," Terry was all said, and the jammer was cut off.

The glow returned, and Cory leaned back into the wounds. Faintly, she heard her father speaking.

"A drop ship is on its way to pick you up."

Dokken whimpered as he laid his head on Ramses' hand. The glow brightened as Cory sent more and more of her energy into her husband.

CHAPTER TWENTY-TWO

The two came at them out of nowhere—ghosts who moved like lightning. The mech had fought valiantly, but the Skrima had gotten through.

Marcie stood her ground, straddling her teammate. Using a short sword to hold the creatures at bay while keeping her pistol aimed, she twisted and contorted her body, refusing to give them an opening. She only needed a millisecond of the Skrima being solid to end their existence.

She was sure she had dialed the JDS to eight—more than that and it could jump from her hand if fired from an awkward position. In her current cobra dance, everything was awkward.

She felt like a ton of bricks hit her when the power of the Etheric disappeared, but Marcie muscled the pistol upward and pulled the trigger. One Skrima disappeared in a cloud of blood and guts.

Yup. Eight.

She adjusted her aim as quickly as she could, but the

Skrima was faster. It caught her wrist and ripped the JDS from her grasp, then turned it, pointed it at her face, and pulled the trigger.

Nothing. It was keyed to Marcie's handprint. She thrust her short blade through the red skin taut across the creature's mid-section, then twisted it and forced the point upward.

She had no idea where the creature's vital organs were, so she scrambled them all. Fist-deep in the rent flesh, she corkscrewed the blade as the Skrima silently mouthed its last words. It fell backwards and pulled Marcie with it, because it had shoved its claws through her flak jacket into her flesh. She worked her way free, tearing the wounds as she did, and fell back to sit on the ground, chest heaving with the strain.

When the power returned she could feel the nanocytes surge through her, and she used the burst of energy to lift the mech suit. When she opened the back, the groan from within told her that he was still alive. She lifted him free before remembering to check for more Skrima.

The one she had scrambled the guts of was standing and facing her. It was covered in blood, but the snarl and the horns told her it was very much alive. Her arms were full as the creature lunged.

The jammer kicked in and the Skrima solidified. Marcie rolled away, feeling the sting as the claws raked through the back of her vest. She ingloriously dropped the warrior, dove forward, rolled, came up with her JDS, and fired. The creature was blown backward, bounced off the upright armor, and fell to the ground. Marcie dialed the weapon back to five, stalked forward, and blasted the thing's head into oblivion.

She accessed her comm device. "Request emergency extract at my coordinates." She left the signal active as she used the first aid kit in her backpack to put field dressings on the gashes across the warrior's chest. His ribs glistened beneath the injuries, and his eyes fluttered as she worked.

Once she got the bleeding stopped, she put her comm device on his chest and climbed into the suit, ignoring the squish from the blood soaking the front.

She powered up the suit, closed it, and fired up the sensors. IR showed clear, and she interfaced with Smedley's map of the planet. The closest Skrima were hundreds of kilometers away. She picked up her teammate and waited. "They're coming," she said reassuringly.

Cory flopped to the side. She had expended everything she had, and three minutes were enough to realize that he was gone.

She curled up next to him and cried. Dokken rolled up against her back to comfort her, but he knew.

Sometimes the only thing one could do was to be there, so he kept his head up and watched. He felt like he had failed once, but he didn't intend to fail her again.

"Cory?" TH called. He waited for two seconds. "Smedley! Where's that shuttle?"

"On its way. ETA is one minute. Marcie's second team is on board the drop ship as part of a tactical leapfrog. They can provide additional assistance."

"One minute, Cory. One more minute." Terry looked at his comm device as if it held the answer. There was no response.

Fitzroy looked out from his mech suit. A private was slumped in the seat, catching a quick nap as the shuttle raced above the terrain. It jerked sideways and headed in a new direction.

"Where are we going?" Fitzroy asked.

"An emergency pickup of Cordelia, Ramses, and Dokken," Smedley replied.

"What happened?"

"Skrima."

Fitzroy and his teammate had come across one pair and shot them from a distance, but they hadn't closed with any others. They were either lucky or unlucky—Fitzroy wasn't sure which.

The drop ship descended rapidly, then flared and landed. When the ramp dropped, Fitzroy hurried out.

He slowed nearly to a stop at the heart-wrenching scene. Dokken shook his head slowly. Cory was drawn into herself.

Fitzroy took a knee next to her. "Come on, Cordelia, let me carry you both into the shuttle." She didn't respond, so the sergeant dug the arms of his suit beneath Ramses' body and carefully lifted him. Cory grabbed her husband and held on as Fitzroy continued to lift.

Cory stood. The blue glow was nowhere to be seen within her sunken eyes. Dokken nuzzled her hip and hand and she followed Fitzroy onto the shuttle, then collapsed on the deck. Fitzroy stood, unsure of where to put Ramses' body. He decided to kneel and cradle the warrior as the rear deck closed.

"Sergeant Fitzroy to Colonel Walton. Sir, Ramses is dead."

Char choked, covered her face, and staggered back into the shuttle. Terry looked up at the sky with glistening eyes, immediately thinking about the first time he met Ramses and the hard time he'd given him. He had never said he was sorry.

And now he couldn't. Terry's mind raced. He lifted the comm device to his mouth. "Continue execution of the mission plan. Smedley, continue to vector our people to the nearest targets. All units, engage at a distance. Do not close with the Skrima. Do not."

He let his finger off the key, watching as if he was moving in slow motion. He could smell the dust within the oppressive heat. Bundin shuffled anxiously.

"What is wrong?" he asked.

"My son-in-law is dead." Terry heard the words, but they sounded like someone else was saying them.

"That is tragic. Are we winning?" The Podder didn't change his tone.

Terry watched his wife sob. *I should comfort her,* he thought as he looked at the small doorway to the other universe. He stared at it until it filled his whole vision. He didn't remember running.

Only arriving. He looked down and saw the JDS in his hand. He was ten yards from the Rift. He braced the pistol against his chest and fired. The pistol hammered into him as the projectile disappeared through the vortex. He fired again. Braced himself afresh and fired again. His chest throbbed in pain. Even through his ballistic vest, the JDS was punishing him.

I deserve it!

Four more times he fired into the Rift, and he screamed with pain and frustration as the Rift started to shrink. Then, without a sound, it disappeared.

"Maybe it wasn't the Benitons who opened the doorway to hell." Terry stood for a few seconds longer, then returned to the drop ship. It took a long time to cover the distance. When he arrived, Bundin was waiting patiently.

"Are we winning, Colonel Walton?" he asked again.

"I think we've won, Bundin, but the cost..." Terry dragged his hand across the Podder's shell as he passed into the cool of the shuttle.

Char had her head between her knees, and Terry sat close enough that their hips touched. He rested his hand on the back of her ballistic vest. In silence, they sat.

Despite what he'd told Bundin, the battle continued.

"Smedley, show the movement of our forces, please," Terry said softly.

Images populated the screen.

"All mech units. I don't expect you to have any rockets when you return to the ship. Smedley will coordinate the firing. This has gone on long enough. And for what it's worth, the Rift is closed. The Skrima have nowhere to go. Be wary. Trapped animals fight the hardest, for they have nothing to lose."

An empty shuttle arrived and Praeter carried the half-human, half-Pricolici inside and placed her on the seats. He didn't know why she was out cold. She was mostly uninjured from the fight with the Skrima.

He left her there and started to back out of the ship, then stopped to check the HUD. Nearest target was forty kilometers away.

"I need a ride, Smedley." He stepped back inside and rolled his armored fist. *Time to go.*

"Would you like to join Colonel Marcie Walton?" Smedley asked. "She appears to be on her own too."

"Too much territory to cover, Smedley. Thanks, but I'll head back into the mix all by myself, as long as you recover me before nightfall. You know me—I'm afraid of the dark." Praeter looked at Christina's prone form. Too bad she'd missed out on a good joke.

"I don't think you are, but sometimes I find human emotions befuddling. Are you afraid now?"

"No. There are Skrima out there that I want to introduce to Mister Pointy." Praeter tapped his railgun.

"Then you shall," Smedley conceded.

Fitzroy wasn't sure what to do. His teammate broke out a body bag from beneath the seat and opened it, and the sergeant looked back and forth between Cory and the bag. He decided it was the right thing to do for Ramses' dignity when the teams boarded after the fight.

"Sergeant Fitzroy. The shuttle is approaching your next drop. The deck will open in fifteen seconds," Smedley reported in a mechanical voice.

With as much grace as he could muster wearing the armored suit, he maneuvered Ramses' body into the bag. The unarmored warrior zipped it closed as the shuttle touched down.

"Take care of them, Dokken," Fitzroy said unnecessarily before ducking and running from the shuttle with the other warrior trailing behind. Both carried their railguns at the ready. The enemy was near.

And they needed to pay.

Fitzroy located the targets on his HUD and adjusted his heading slightly as he ran.

The rockets over his shoulder popped out, and two of them fired. In his HUD, he watched them head toward two pairs of Skrima that were going to be on the receiving end of Federation technology. The rockets impacted without a sound that they could hear, and the IR signatures of the targets disappeared.

Fitzroy slowed to a walk and used arm signals to show where the Skrima were hiding. No longer walking in circles, they'd quickly adapted to their new circumstances.

Maybe they knew the doorway to their own dimension was closed. Maybe they didn't care.

Neither did Fitzroy. *Watch my back,* he told his teammate.

He adjusted his position, aimed, and sent withering fire from his oversized railgun through a small hill into a depression beyond. When Fitzroy started to run, the only thing he could see was the devastated look on Cory's face.

He charged into the gap where the wounded Skrima were ready to make their last stand.

Fine, he thought, and with a series of well-aimed bursts he foiled their plans for a glorious death.

Terry's shuttle cruised toward the nearest IR targets. The ship descended, and Terry checked his pistol as the rear deck lowered. Plenty of ammunition remained.

He dialed the JDS back to seven and walked into the humidity of a small rainforest. "Where are they, Smedley?" Terry asked.

Bundin hurried after him. The Podder was carrying two railguns.

"One hundred meters at one o'clock to your current heading."

Terry adjusted to his right and started looking for an opening.

"Fifty meters. One is behind the largest tree, and the second one is farther into the rainforest."

Terry checked overhead to make sure the tree wouldn't fall on him.

"I'll watch for a runner, Bundin. You take out the target behind that tree." The Podder aimed and fired, zigzagging the lines of devastation as the darts tore through the trunk and into the creature beyond. The tree cracked and slowly fell into the smaller trees next to it, taking them with it on its way to the marshy ground and sending a wide spray in all directions when it hit.

Terry took one step and found Char next to him. She carried a pistol in each hand. Her eyes were puffy and glistening, and more tears threatened to fall. She clenched her teeth as she looked around TH for the next target.

"Where did it go, Smedley?" Terry asked.

"Bundin's fire was effective and eliminated both targets," Smedley reported.

Terry took one last look at the fallen tree before turning on his heel. Bundin slopped through a puddle, then backed up and went through it a second time.

Charumati stopped to watch him, tilting her head as the Podder splashed in the water. He turned completely around to put each of his stumpy legs in. Dripping, he continued to the drop ship.

"Why?" Char asked softly.

"We don't have water like this on my planet, nor on the ship, nor on the space station."

"It's the little things," Terry whispered into his wife's hair. "The little things that make life worth living. Let's finish this and go home. It's time to mourn. It's time to talk with our family back on Earth. It's time for a lot of things that don't include getting people killed."

"What about Ten?"

"We'll get to him, but not now. We need to go home. We

need more mech suits. I won't go into combat again without everyone armored up."

He didn't have to say that he'd never contemplated that the nanocytes would be rendered nonfunctional and make the warriors too vulnerable.

"We won't face a superior enemy on Home World, but we will face humans. We saw too many humans meet their end on Earth. I'm okay never seeing another human die." The group climbed aboard, and the rear deck rose and locked into place.

"Smedley?"

"Mop-up operations are underway," the general reported.

"Let's pick up our people and get the hell off this godforsaken planet."

Marcie ran as fast as the suit would allow as she hunted down the last two Skrima. She was tired from not having her nanocytes active, but she was willing to overlook that to ensure that the Skrima would be solid when she finally cornered them.

They were running—the first she'd seen or heard of that—but they were slow too. In the short sprints they were speed-of-thought fast, but over the distance they were running out of energy.

Marcie caught them in the open and didn't waste any time before firing a long stream of hypervelocity darts. The projectiles raked across the Skrima and they turned and howled in their anguish at her, then thrust their heads back to rage at the sky.

"I never liked shooting an enemy in the back. Thanks for being so accommodating," Marcie told them as she sent a final burst their way. The creatures blew apart, as was usual when a stream of hypervelocity darts impacted living flesh.

She shouldered her oversized weapon, verified no further targets on her HUD, and activated her comm system.

"Colonel Walton reporting sector is clear."

"The planet is clear. Picking you up in five, Marcie," Terry replied tiredly.

CHAPTER TWENTY-THREE

The *War Axe*

Char rushed across the hangar bay and waited impatiently for the rear deck of her daughter's drop ship to open. The warriors in the mechs moved to the side, parked their units, and started to climb out.

No one talked. Many were injured, but they had started to heal once the final Skrima had been eliminated and Ted shut off his satellite weapon for the last time.

Ted and Ankh stood near the hatch leading to the interior of the *War Axe*. They looked impassive, but the fact that they were there and not in Ted's lab spoke to their feelings.

Terry moved through the warriors, checking on the injured and shaking hands with the teams. Marcie followed him. He turned to her as if to ask her to take care of it, but he couldn't. Every member of Bad Company's Direct Action Branch was his family.

"Join Char. I'll be along shortly," he told her.

She didn't move. "No."

Terry had given an order. He didn't understand.

"You join your wife and daughter. *I'll* be along shortly." Marcie hugged TH and gently brushed him out of the way so she could carry on with the post-combat leadership engagement.

Christina appeared, and Marcie nodded to her to come over.

Terry excused himself and strode briskly across the *Axe's* hangar bay. *Never run. It upsets the troops.*

Char was holding a nearly catatonic Cordelia as four warriors carried out the body bag. From all the engagements, all the blood shed on Benitus Seven, only one body bag.

Once up a time Terry Henry would have considered that a blessing—to fight such an enemy and only lose one of his people—but not anymore. He looked across the hangar bay. The entirety of his combat force was there. If he lost a person a week, they would all be gone within a year.

He felt guilty for thinking he needed to recruit more warriors. Train them and then put them onto foreign shores. The Marines' Hymn played in his mind.

> *From the Halls of Montezuma*
> *To the shores of Tripoli;*
> *We fight our country's battles*
> *In the air, on land, and sea;*

> *First to fight for right and freedom*

And to keep our honor clean;
We are proud to claim the title
Of United States Marine.

Exporting justice to the universe, Terry thought. *First to fight for right and freedom. Of course, but the freedom of others, and it comes at a price that we are willing to pay. Glory to those who stand between the oppressors and the oppressed, for they will know both honor and death. They will know freedom through the eyes of the free.*

When Terry reached his family, Kim, Kae, and Auburn were already standing close to Char and Cory. Kae looked for Marcie, frowning when he saw her at the other end of the bay, then looked at his dad and *knew* she was there so Terry could do the right thing and be with his wife and daughter. Kae nodded in understanding.

Terry wrapped his arms around Char and Cory, but the only thing he could think of to say was, "I don't have the words." They cried as the Bad Company stood in silence and watched.

Micky breathed softly. The mood around the table was sullen. Terry looked at his wife, who looked down at the table. Christina stood up.

"I got this." The others in the room—Joseph, Petricia, Shonna, Merrit, Kae, Kim, Marcie, Auburn, Fitzroy, Dokken, Bundin, Ankh, and Ted—looked up at her. "Smedley, patch me through to my father."

After a short delay, Nathan's face appeared as a holographic projection above the center of the table. He smiled when he saw Christina, but then he panned his view around the room. "What happened?"

Christina spoke. "Cory's husband Ramses was killed on Benitus Seven. The Rift has been closed, and the Skrima have been eliminated. We have the schematics to build the Etheric power supplies, and we have unlimited access to the space station as long as we stay off the planet."

"Mission success," Nathan replied dryly. "Son of a bitch. Please accept Ecaterina's and my sincere condolences. It's my fault for sending you out there."

Terry pounded a fist on the table and glared at the projection. "It's not your fault, Nathan! We set out on this path a long, long time ago when we first formed the Force de Guerre. All of us have suffered. Just tell us that it's worth it, Nathan…that our sacrifices matter."

"More than you can ever know, TH, and that's on me. We'll set up an honorarium as a testament to what Bad Company's Direct Action Branch has done—a museum in the heart of the Federation, and we'll call it the Price of Freedom. Everyone who dies in service to the Bad Company will have a place. Every system liberated will get a dedication." Nathan stopped, but no one filled the void with their voice. "Unfortunately, both lists are growing."

"That they are," Terry said as he leaned back in his chair, his energy spent.

"I'd like to say something," Ted said.

All eyes turned to him, and he looked down as he spoke. "I've known Ramses a long time, but I didn't *know* him. I don't *know* anyone really, besides Felicity, and she says I should make an effort to know the others. Believe me, I have expended a great deal of energy on that endeavor, but to no avail. I concede that I will never understand people, but I accept that that's okay because of people like Cordelia and Ramses. Even Terry Henry and Charumati.

"We have all committed of our own free will to this ideal that Bethany Anne has for a greater universe where people can live free. It started on Earth and continues right here, nine thousand, seven hundred and fourteen light years away. No matter what, I'm in. We're doing the right thing, and Felicity thinks so, too."

Ted stopped talking. Ankh glanced at him, face impassive.

Christina remained standing. "Anything else?" she asked.

"It's good to see you," Nathan replied, feeling selfish once the words had left his mouth. "Is there a chance that these 'Skrima,' as you call them, will return?"

Christina didn't have an answer.

Joseph raised his hand, and Christina pointed to him. "I was able to briefly touch their minds. They are intelligent, but think differently from us. They consider us as a blight, and would not have surrendered. They will return, but when and where I don't know. I do know that they can control the Rift. If they open another portal to our universe, we have to stop them and close it."

"I will send out a Federation-wide alert with all the data related to the Rift and the Skrima. Good job, people. I know that won't bring Ramses back, but as I keep saying, you've saved a lot of lives. The miniaturized Etheric power supply will fund the Bad Company from now to the end of time, and every single space vehicle will have at least one on board along with the micro-gate technology Ted is working on."

"All hail Ted," Smedley interjected.

Terry shook his head.

Ted fidgeted, but smiled as he looked into his lap. "The IICS is ready," Ted said, still looking down. "You need to send a number of units to Earth. I have a list prepared of who will get the first ones."

"Of course. We'll see that gets done the second we have the units in hand. And congratulations—that is a huge step for us. The Bad Company, shrinking the universe one discovery at a time."

No one cheered, and Christina looked uncomfortable.

"I want to talk with Uncle Gene," Kimber said softly.

"Me too," Kae added.

"We need to talk with our grandkids. They need to know that their father... They need to know the great things that he did." Terry stood. "Next time we'll have drinks on the table, because we toast the fallen. Always. Here's to Ramses, and Gomez, and those who have gone before and those who will follow."

Everyone in the captain's conference room stood and raised a hand in the air. "Hear, hear," they intoned.

"Hear, hear," Nathan replied.

"We're heading straight back to Keeg Station, then liberty until we have enough suits for everyone. Please make it so, Nathan."

"What about Ten? You're close to Home World."

"Ten isn't going anywhere, and maybe we can bring some of the captives back with us to help liberate their birthplace."

"Sounds like a plan, TH. Lowell out."

Spires Harbor

"I'll be damned," Timmons said. "Amazeballs!"

"I have to admit that it is miraculous," Felicity drawled, watching the shipyard grow. "One day. It's been *one day*."

"But it's been a damn good day, with an army of motivated workers and all the raw materials anyone could ask for."

"Cool your jets, Timmons. Dion, when will we run out of construction materials for the new shipyard?"

"Four days, Madam Director," the AI answered.

"Your boys are hungry." Felicity focused on one side of the construction where the first tie-in was being finished—one of the spider's legs.

The initial project would have room for eight starships. Once they gathered more raw materials and the power to process it they would start enclosing a main section, half of which would be metal and the other half powered shields. Zero-gee, but breathable atmosphere—the best of both construction worlds.

Timmons pulled Sue to him and hugged her. "We couldn't have done it without you."

"Because I turned into a werewolf while getting mobbed? You have got to be shitting me."

"The catalytic moment that changed the course of destiny," Timmons said in a low voice with his hand over his heart. "And you know you love how they defer to you as you walk by."

Sue chuckled. "I do like that."

"I do, too," Felicity added.

"Next up, mine the asteroid belt. That's a whole new project plan." Timmons blew out his cheeks as the list of needs started taking shape in his mind.

"We need more project managers," Sue said.

"I know two werewolves who would be perfect for it."

"Char will *lose* her mind if the entire pack stays here, although Shonna would love to get back to engineering— and Merrit. What the hell does he do again?"

"I thought he was a chemist, but I don't remember. It's been so long since he's done anything other than being man-candy for his woman."

Sue slapped Timmons on the arm. "Is that how you think of me?"

"I was thinking that's how you thought of me!" He smiled to show his perfect white teeth.

"Char was right about you." Sue stepped away from her mate, crossing her arms and glaring.

"What do you mean?"

"Maybe we need to cut off a hand and rein you back in."

"Whoa! Enough hand-cutting talk." Timmons grimaced, flinching as if it had just happened. "That hurt a shitload and it sucked like you can't believe, hopping around on three legs. Don't even joke about that."

Timmons turned away and Sue hugged him from behind. "I'll protect you from the alpha," she purred, and he grasped her arms where they came around his chest.

"As long as we do right by them it'll be good. Look at this shipyard: give us a couple weeks and the Bad Company's shipbuilding and repair branch will be open for business. We may have to build a gate to bring in more customers and trade. Make this a real stop on the highway to progress."

"I'm not sure Nathan would like that. He likes having his secrets, like Keeg Station."

"He can build another station in the middle of nowhere. If we're going to make this place ours, it needs to be mainstream. What do you think, Felicity?"

"I think I miss my husband."

Sue slid one hand down Timmons' back to grab his butt. "I know what she means," she whispered in his ear.

"And I agree," Felicity drawled. "I loved how San Francisco was constantly growing. Keeg Station in the Dren Cluster is open for business. Come one, come all."

The *War Axe*

The *War Axe* crossed the event horizon into the space beside Keeg Station.

"Hoods," Micky said. The bridge crew released their hoods and helped them retract into the backs of their collars. "It's nice to be home."

Terry and Char looked at the station that loomed large in the viewscreens which made up the front wall of the ship's bridge.

"Home," Char whispered. Cory stood beside her, gazing out through vacant eyes.

Terry cupped their faces in his hands. "Home is anywhere you are." Cory tried to nod, but stopped and looked at her feet.

"Cordelia Dawn we named you, because on the day of your birth we lost the chief of the tribe. With each person's passing a new day arises; a void needs to be filled. We pack that space with our memories and a sound way ahead, because time will always move forward, second after second. We are along for the ride, no matter what."

Char hugged her daughter with one arm as Terry caressed their cheeks.

"Home is anywhere you are," Micky offered, tapping the arm of the captain's chair.

Char looked up and smiled for the first time in days.

The End of Price of Freedom, Book 3 of The Bad Company.

If you like this book, please leave a review. Reviews buoy my spirits and stoke the fires of creativity.

Don't stop now! Keep turning the pages as Craig & Michael talk about their thoughts on this book and the overall project called the Age of Expansion (and if you haven't read the eleven-book prequel, the Terry Henry Walton Chronicles, now is a great time to take a look).
Terry, Char, and the rest of the Bad Company's Direct Action Branch will return in Liberation.

AUTHOR NOTES - CRAIG MARTELLE

FEBRUARY 14, 2018

I can't thank you enough for continuing to read this series. Terry Henry Walton and the fine characters who surround him have become a part of my world. I hope they've become a part of yours as well. Honor. Courage. Commitment. Something we can all live for and be proud of.

Thank you, Tracey Byrnes for the name that I used for the representative from the Home World captives. Also to Tim Adams—he's been reading Terry Henry since the beginning and we hadn't gotten him into a book yet, so I remedied that with this volume. You'll remember him from Monty Python fame. I had to use the line, although I left off the airspeed velocity of a laden swallow thing because I find the math befuddling.

Staci Armstrong offered Rowan as the name for Brice's girlfriend, but it was another one of the captives who was introduced to the spice of life. Thanks, Staci. And for Rowan's acolyte, we'll call him Chris-bo-Runner on behalf of Diane Brenner. She offered her son to be sacrificed on the author's altar of posterity.

Thanks, Diane! Party on.

We received a one-star review for Blockade from a person who felt that I was talking down to him in my author notes. Authors should never reply to reviews on Amazon. That's a safe policy to embrace, but all I can say is that was not my intent and would never be my intent. If someone hates my book, then I question my marketing and how it got into that person's hand. I don't ever question the reader or look down on them. I appreciate everyone who picks up one of my books and reads it all the way to the end. That's boss! Or groovy, or a myriad of era-specific terms. Thank you for reading my books and I hope you enjoy them. Without you, most of these books wouldn't exist. Without readers, there is very little reason to keep writing.

I have gotten such overwhelming support from the readers that I am humbled and incredibly grateful. Here's to you!

In Chapter Sixteen you'll find a bit about Nathan meeting a human trader with his Yollin and Balorean companions. I lifted that bit directly from Tom Dublin's first addition to the Age of Expansion—*Gravity Storm* in the exciting new series, Shadow Vanguard. There is a great deal of crossover in the universe, and I wanted to highlight Tommy D because he is a stellar member of the team.

What happens when Nathan tries to recruit this team? Read *Gravity Storm* to find out.

I just got back from London. There are some authors over there! I got to meet some fine people, including Tommy D, Erika Everest, and Natale Roberts—good people joining us to write in the Kurtherian Gambit Universe. So many great stories are coming.

I also got to meet the ship captain's namesake, Micky Cocker and her husband Russ. Micky is there whenever I need an opinion on anything I write. She'll read it and let me know how it works, without delay, allowing me the freedom and foresight to keep moving forward. Such wonderful people all. It makes flying across nine time zones worthwhile. I have to admit that I was tired the entire time I was in London, all five days. But the incredible people who came to the show appreciated it. They were unfailingly kind in their words and deeds.

What else is going on? We did complete new typography on the Terry Henry Walton Chronicles and are relaunching the series with a big bang from February 26th to March 2nd, 2018. Our goal is to bring new readers on board, welcome them to Michael's fantastic universe that is The Kurtherian Gambit.

That's it—break's over, back to writing the next book. Peace, fellow humans.

Please join my Newsletter (www.craigmartelle.com – please, please, please sign up!), or you can follow me on Facebook since you'll get the same opportunity to pick up the books for only 99 cents on that first day they are published.

If you liked this story, you might like some of my other books. You can join my mailing list by dropping by my website **www.craigmartelle.com** or if you have any comments, shoot me a note at craig@craigmartelle.com. I am always happy to hear from people who've read my work. I try to answer every email I receive.

If you liked the story, please write a short review for me on Amazon. I greatly appreciate any kind words; even one or two sentences go a long way. The number of reviews an ebook receives greatly improves how well it does on Amazon.

Amazon – www.amazon.com/author/craigmartelle

Facebook – www.facebook.com/authorcraigmartelle

My web page – www.craigmartelle.com

Twitter – www.twitter.com/rick_banik

Thank you for reading *Price of Freedom*, the third book in an entire new series!

AUTHOR NOTES - MICHAEL ANDERLE

FEBRUARY 17, 2018

Thank you ALWAYS for not only reading this story, but reading all of the way to the back and through to these author notes, as well ;-)

I happened to be in London at the same time as Craig, and met those amazing people he mentioned (and many more including Abby-Lynn Knorr (Oriceran), Meg Cowly (Oriceran), Micky Cocker (Kurtherian and others, but we are keeping her here), Dan Willcocks (Age of Madness – Kurtherian) and of course Martha Carr (Oriceran) as well as many others. It was a wonderful time and (while I don't think any of the other authors outside of those mentioned above read my stuff) *HELLO* from over the pond!

Just in case they do read our stuff.

This latest week, we released TWO books on Valentine's day. Bethany Anne's book 21 (and the end to the Kurtherian Gambit saga. Her next book is The Kurtherian Endgame.) Also, Dawn Arrives, the fourth and last book in The Second Dark Ages.

In those two, the lovers reunite.

I was the last author leaving the time I call the second dark ages (between WWDE and when Bethany Anne and group surround the Earth with the BYPS system.) We (Craig Martelle, Justin Sloan and myself) wrote twenty-two books during that time with Craig and Justin writing eighteen.

I wrote four… and half of those four books Ell Leigh Clarke helped me with!

I just want to say KUDOS to those guys for making this age work out, and giving all of us a playground to work with.

If you aren't aware, Terry Henry was a character back in my original series who stayed on Earth, and his wife and child were killed during WWDE (World's Worst Day Ever) and the time around that event. I had to ask Craig to write a series which was during this post-apocalyptic timeframe because I had learned my lesson.

Don't leave big gaps in the timeline, fans are *no Bueno* on that stuff.

Now, leading up to THE BIG RELEASE of these two major series and the ONE major event so many readers wished to see (Michael and Bethany Anne getting back together) I received a LOT of questions, but one was at the top…

"Which book do I read first? Life Goes on (TKG21) or Dawn Arrives (TSDA04)?"

I answered, "21 then 4!"

Apparently, I should have answered the other way around. Why? Because that sumbitch MURPHY got ahold of my plans and puckered them up.

Now, I wrote book 21 first. Had it go through editing,

worked it all out and it was ready to go. I wrote (with Ell) the second book because if ANYTHING should happen to the timeline, then Bethany Anne needed to drop first on Valentine's day.

It was important. Not only to the fans, but to me personally.

We (and by 'we' I mean Zen Master Walking™ Stephen Campbell) released book 21 first. Ten minutes later, he pushed the button to release Dawn Arrives to make sure everything was copacetic.

One hour later, Dawn Arrives pops up on the store for fans to start purchasing and Life Goes On is saying it is 'publishing' which means the book is supposed to be released to the servers for purchase by the fans.

It is *supposed* to mean that.

I won't bore you with the details (go to either the Facebook page, or the Facebook group for the gory details, the offers to storm a certain businesses offices and other myriad and often funny comments) but Life Goes On didn't show up until the morning of the 15th...

DAMMIT!

It just goes to show that no matter how many weeks you work towards a goal, it can always be screwed up at the last moment and the only thing to do is smile and work hard on the next project.

While you grumble under your breath and say AWFUL things about computer servers and stupid processes that don't work properly. I'm personally hoping the servers weren't monitoring my speech.

Cause the next book will take a week, I'm sure.

THANK YOU for supporting all of us here in The

Kurtherian Gambit. We have more (and more and more) stories we want to tell, including one about a big-assed ship.

We (Craig and I) think you will enjoy that one quite a bit.

Ad Aeternitatem!

Michael Anderle

Craig Martelle's other books (listed by series)

Terry Henry Walton Chronicles (co-written with Michael Anderle) – a post-apocalyptic paranormal adventure

Gateway to the Universe (co-written with Justin Sloan & Michael Anderle) – this book transitions the characters from the Terry Henry Walton Chronicles to The Bad Company

The Bad Company (co-written with Michael Anderle) – a military science fiction space opera

End Times Alaska (also available in audio) – a Permuted Press publication – a post-apocalyptic survivalist adventure

The Free Trader – a Young Adult Science Fiction Action Adventure

Cygnus Space Opera – A Young Adult Space Opera (set in the Free Trader universe)

Darklanding (co-written with Scott Moon) – a Space Western

Rick Banik – Spy & Terrorism Action Adventure

Become a Successful Indie Author – a non-fiction work

Enemy of my Enemy (co-written with Tim Marquitz) – a galactic alien military space opera

Superdreadnought (co-written with Tim Marquitz) – a military space opera

Metal Legion (co-written with Caleb Wachter) - a military space opera

End Days (co-written with E.E. Isherwood) – a post-apocalyptic adventure

Mystically Engineered (co-written with Valerie Emerson) – dragons in space

Monster Case Files (co-written with Kathryn Hearst) – a young-adult cozy mystery series

For a complete list of books from Craig, please see www. craigmartelle.com

Made in the USA
Columbia, SC
03 March 2023

13270110R00167